King Rush Publishing LLC Presents

THE GANGSTER

VS.

THE PREACHER

A Novel By

Frederick B. Rush Jr.

This novel is a work of fiction. All names, characters, places and incidents are products of the author's imagination. Any resemblance to actual events or persons, living or dead, is purely coincidental.

Scriptures are taken from the King James Version unless otherwise marked.

ISBN# 978-0-692-87382-3
Christian Fiction

TABLE OF CONTENTS

FOREWARD

As Frederick's wife of six years, I have witnessed many of his most recent memorable moments. One of these moments entailed his decision to use some of his life experiences as a testimonial to others and for the glory of God. Indeed Frederick has poured out some of life's many encounters with good and evil in this inspirational fiction novel. These happenings have helped him develop a powerful and meaningful message in this story of a young man striving for holiness while living in a world full of sin.

Jacob, a young man filled with faith and a genuine love for God, tries to stay on the straight and narrow path. But when he wants to do good, evil always awaits him. "I find then a law, that, when I would do good, evil is present with me." (Romans 7:21).

Take this powerful journey with Jacob, as author Frederick Rush gives vivid examples of the pressures of this world in this engaging novel. *The Gangster Vs. The Preacher* exudes transparency with real life issues as it pertains to temptations. "There hath no temptation taken you but such as is common to man..." (1 Corinthians 10:13). Jacob, as well as many people today, faces life-changing decisions that could either bless or curse his future. Mike, a gangster, and his affiliates try to lure Jacob to the dark side with drugs, money, and violence. On the contrary, Pastor Mark, a true man of God, encourages Jacob to walk out his faith in Christ Jesus. Just when Jacob begins to overcome evil, the plot thickens. The author gives shocking surprises that will keep the reader engaged in this purposeful story.

Readers, both believing and unbelieving, may find themselves relating to Jacob's experiences throughout the book. Although the story of Jacob is fictional, it gives light to the struggles and victories both young people and adults face in society today. Frederick connects with his audience by using common day issues and terms the average reader can easily understand. Whether a young adult or older individual, one will surely be encouraged by the book's overall message of deliverance, courage, and victory in Christ.

Rebecca P. Rush
Author of *From Pain to Promise:
Discovering Your Purposeful Wait!*
Wife, Friend, and Business Partner

ACKNOWLEDGEMENTS

First, I would like to give thanks to Jesus Christ, my Lord and Savior. You are the author and finish to my faith. I would not even be here doing what I am doing if it was not for your grace and mercy upon my life.

I would like to thank my beautiful and lovely wife, Rebecca Rush, for never giving up on me and allowing me to be me. You make me stronger and help me be a better man day by day, and most of all, you have a very powerful walk with the Lord.

To my son, Josiah King Rush, you are the whole reason why I do this, because I want to build the wealth for you to pass down to my grandchildren. I would never want you to experience the struggles that I've been through. Always walk with Jesus and follow your own heart. Never follow another man unless they follow Jesus.

My mother, Gail Holt, you are the other special woman in my life. There is nothing that I would not do for you. You made me be the man that I am today by teaching me the Word of God in my younger days and letting me know to trust in God and not worry about things that come in my life trying to stop me. You showed me how to keep moving forward and to be strong for other people that may need me. Thank you for that.

To my father, Frederick B. Holt Sr., for being here for me day by day. I can always call you for spiritual counseling and you will give me the Word from the Lord. Thank you for letting me know to stick with Jesus and never turn my back on God. You showed me that we all make mistakes but can put them behind us and move on in life if we go to God and ask for His forgiveness.

To my older sister, Sharone Rush, thanks for always teaching me to be responsible in my earlier days.

To my older sister, Taria Lucas, thanks for teaching me how to tie my shoes at the age of three years old and showing me how to cross the street. I can never forget those days. It all seems like just yesterday.

To my older sister, Kendra Rush, thanks for making me tougher and coming up to the schools to fight hand to hand with me against other people when they were thinking it was sweet.

To my little brother, Jeremiah Rush, my right-hand man thanks for always keeping me sharp. We were always competing with each other. We played video games to try to be better than each other all the time. And when we got older we became closer to each other. To God I give the glory.

To my little sister, Camilla Holt, you have a good heart and would look out and give me your last five dollars. Keep helping people the way you do and God will bless you sooner than you think. Trust in Jesus. Never put your

4

faith in any other gods because Jesus is the only God you need.

My little brother, Damon Rush, I know you're no longer here on earth but I can hear you right now asking me when we are going to do the movie for the book. Don't worry, the movie is going to be on point and will be out soon. This book was partly your idea because you told me that I should start writing. You knew I would be a writer and upcoming film director because you believed in me. I love you and miss you, brother, and I will always make sure I let people know who you were as my little brother.

To my little brother, Emmanuel Rush, thanks for always looking up to me as a big brother. You came a long way from making me make you do your homework before you played video games. After that you were in math challenges and the whole nine yards. You turned out to be a very smart man and learned how to work hard in life.

To my baby sister, Grace Holt, thank you for always asking me questions and learning from me, because you were helping me learn the whole time when I was teaching you. You turned out to be a very beautiful young woman. Just know when times get hard to call on the Lord.

I would like to also thank: all my nieces and nephews, my Holt family on my father's side and my Rush and Lucas family on my mother's side, my in-laws Clarity, Rachel, and Harmony Govan, and Josh Palmer, my true friends that I grew up with and that have been with me from day one, all my schoolteachers who took the time to work with me from the time I was in kindergarten until my six years in college, and all my coworkers that I was cool with that worked with me throughout my career on every job I've worked at.

A special thank you to my father and mother-in-law, Bishop Earl and Prophetess Maria Palmer, who are also my pastors. Finally, thanks to Ministers Mark Broady and Greg Locke for allowing me to put you on my book cover, and to my entire Brand New Life Christian Center family. To everyone else who helped make this possible for me today, if I forgot your name please forgive me. Blame my mind, not my heart.

DEDICATION

This book is dedicated with love and memory
to my little brother

R.I.P. Damon L. Rush
7/20/1985 – 1/29/2011

Thank you for all the times we shared together as brothers. You were one of the realest people who ever walked on the face of this earth. You are gone but you will never be forgotten. I will work harder to bring wealth to your children. Do not worry. Uncle Fred got them. May you continue to rest in peace.

FREDERICK B. RUSH JR.

Chapter 1

TRAINING UP A CHILD

Proverbs 22:6 KJV

Train up a child in the way he should go: and when he is old, he will not depart from it.

On September 5, 1979 Hannah Justice gave birth to her son, Jacob B. Justice, Jr., who she was pregnant with by her late husband, Jacob B. Justice, Sr. When Hannah gave birth to Jacob she was the happiest woman in the world. She could not help but think about how happy her husband would have been to see his son born. The very same day Jacob Jr. was born, Jacob B. Justice, Sr. died in a car crash that involved 12 other deaths. The accident occurred because of a drunk driver who was driving on the wrong side of the road. Jacob Sr. had been on his way to the hospital to witness the birth of his son. Instead, he went home to be in glory with the Lord and was now in heaven. After giving birth to Jacob, Hannah realized how difficult her life could get, but she knew that she could do all things through Jesus Christ as she was a firm believer who put her faith in God.

Hannah worked two full-time jobs. One of her jobs was working at a bank as a teller. Her second job was working as a sales clerk at a suit company that sold all different types of tailor-made suits. Hannah worked extra hours to make ends meet for her and Jacob. She was raising him as a single mother with help from her best friend, Carla, who was also Jacob's godmother. Carla would look after Jacob and let him watch Bible cartoons while Hannah worked her two full-time jobs. Carla also owned a daycare service and watched other children.

*****

Five years quickly passed by and it was September 5, 1984. At five years old, Jacob was filled with God's Word and would always ask his mother questions about the Bible. He always was a great listener of things he heard. On Sunday he'd heard Pastor Mark saying that Jesus wept so he asked Hannah why.

"Jacob, Jesus wept because of Martha and Mary's unbelief," Hannah explained with tears in her eyes.

"Oh, okay," Jacob replied not fully understanding what this meant.

"Time to sing happy birthday, Jacob," said Hannah. Jacob looked at his mother with joy and blew out his five candles. As he opened his gifts, he unwrapped a children's Bible that played audio scriptures and had pictures. After opening all his gifts he picked up his Bible and stood in front of the mirror in his bedroom, pretending to be a preacher that spoke the Word from the Lord.

Later on that day, Jacob asked his mother if he could go outside and play with his friends, and she agreed. Once outside Jacob found his friend, Corey. They played with their toys and had fun all day until it was time for them to go in and eat dinner.

"See you tomorrow, Corey" said Jacob as he walked into his house. Jacob sat at the dinner table to eat with his mother. Before eating, he said grace and thanked the Lord for the food that was placed on the table.

"Hey Mom, how come I don't have a daddy like Corey does? He told me that he sits and eats dinner with his mom and his dad." Hannah looked at Jacob and saw that he had tears in his eyes. She could tell that he really wanted to know what happened to his dad, but felt that he was too young to understand the full truth now.

"Your dad went to be with the Lord in heaven and he is an angel now. I promise you son, when you get older I will let you know all that you need to know about your father. Just know that your father was a true man of God. He was a man with a lot of power and authority from God," said Hannah with tears in her eyes as she kissed Jacob on the head.

"I love you, Mom. You are the best mom I could ever have." Jacob smiled, kissed his mother on the cheek, and hugged her. Then they went to bed and he slept in her arms.

*****

11

When Hannah and Jacob woke up the next morning they got dressed and went to church to hear a Word from the Lord. Pastor Mark was speaking about the trials that happen in our lives every day, like losing a job and finding a new job. He was using the King James Version of the Bible, and was speaking from Matthew 6:33, which tells us to seek God and his righteousness first, and then all things will be given to us.

Pastor Mark then went on about how people of today depend on things from the world more than God himself.

"Amen!" came a loud shout from the congregation. "You better preach, pastor! I know that's right!" stated Hannah from the middle of the church. She began to worship the Lord in the middle of Pastor Mark's sermon. "Hallelujah, oh Hallelujah! Thank you, Jesus. We give you praise!" Then the whole congregation started to praise and worship the Lord as Jacob sat, looking at his mother as if she was going crazy.

When he had finished his sermon, Pastor Mark spoke to the congregation. "Thank you, Jesus. This is the day that the Lord has made and we need to just rejoice. You never know what God will do in his house. I had no intentions on making this service today become a worship service said Pastor Mark. When God is in control you have to allow Him to do what He does best and that's dealing with our hearts."

Music resounds from the altar as the choir starts to sing. They are singing a beautiful song, glorifying the Holy

Spirit: *Jesus, You are Lord, and Lord of the world. Where would we be if there were no You? Jesus, You are Lord. Jesus, You are Lord.*

Pastor Mark turned to address his congregation once again. "If there is anyone here today that does not know Jesus as their Lord then please come up to this altar now."

Four young men came to the altar with heavy tears in their eyes. They took the guns from their waists and laid them down then fell on their knees as they continued to cry.

"Hallelujah!" Pastor Mark shouted. "My God, My God, You are so good! Now, you young men, repeat after me."

They did what they were told and sincerely repeated the words. "Dear Lord Jesus, come into my life. I know that I am a sinner and I want the new life from the highest, God. I do believe you died on the cross for my sins and then rose from the dead. Forgive me, Jesus and make me a new person. Make me holy like you. Thank you for restoring my life. I will live for you from this day on. In Jesus' name, amen."

Jacob watched the four young men as they walked back to their seats. The congregation began to applaud the four young men that gave their lives to the Lord. Pastor Mark asked the deacons of the church to get rid of the guns that had been laid at the altar.

Then he called Jacob up to the altar to give him a word; a prophecy. "Don't think God will not use you at a young age, because he can, Jacob," said Pastor Mark. "I see you at a young age spreading the Word of God in your school and at your camp. You have to just continue listening to your mom and do what is right unto God as well as your mother. I knew your dad and I watched him preach many times, and if it was not for God using your dad to save me I would not be here to speak to you today, Jacob," he said. "I love you, Jacob. Always be a good kid. I know you are too young to understand most of these things but some day you will."

Hannah sat in the middle of the church watching Pastor Mark speak to her son with tears of joy in her eyes. Pastor Mark then asked Jacob to do the benediction. Jacob agreed and, before he began, asked that the congregation have all minds and hearts cleared.

"Dear God, thank you for waking us up this morning to make it to church and hear your Word. We thank you for your Spirit that came on us and please let everyone make it home okay. Thank you, in the name of Jesus. Amen." The congregation clapped and Pastor Mark then dismissed everyone from church.

Chapter 2

GROWING UP AS A YOUNG TEEN

Psalms 119:9 KJV

Wherewithal shall a young man cleanse his way? By taking heed thereto according to thy Word.

Several years had passed and Jacob was now at the age where he could begin making his own choices in his life. Jacob walked through the streets while eating a Butterfinger candy bar and looked up to see two men fist-fighting. One man was big and buff while the other was very small and skinny. The skinny man was beating the buff man very badly and telling him that he only had a few more days to come up with the rest of his money. He looked up and saw Jacob watching, then began walking toward him.

"Hey, what's cracking, little man? My name is Mike. What's your name?"

"My mom told me to never to talk to strangers," Jacob said to the skinny man.

"Your mother is a smart woman," replied Mike before handing him a business card. "I want you to call me. I have a job for you if you want one. Make sure you speak with your mother about it first, then we can meet."

"Why did you beat that guy up so bad?"

Mike looked at Jacob with a smile on his face. "That man needed that done to him."

Jacob walked away with one last look at Mike. He could hear his mother calling him. "Coming now, Mom," Jacob yelled down to the other end of the street.

Jacob finally reached home to have dinner with his mother.

"Jacob, why were you down the street talking to that guy? He seems like trouble and I already told you not to talk to strangers. You took too long coming back from the store, son, and you had me beginning to worry about you."

"I am sorry, Mom. He offered me a job though."

"That sounds good. When can this guy come over for dinner and talk to me a little more about this job he claims that he has for you? How will you be able to contact him?" Jacob reached in his pants pocket and handed Hannah the business card that he got from Mike.

The next day, which was Friday the 13th, Hannah called Mike at the number on the business card. Mike answered the phone after the second ring.

"Hey, how are you? I hope you are having a blessed day as this is the day the Lord has made," Hannah said to Mike before asking him about the job that he told Jacob he had.

"Yeah, I have a job for him at my barber shop cleaning up hair around the stylists' chairs. He will be getting paid $4 for each chair after every person gets their hair cut."

"How many chairs does your shop have?" Hannah asked.

"We have a total of eight chairs in my shop and each chair sees around 14 people a day."

"Four dollars times eight is thirty-two, and thirty-two times fourteen is 448, so you are telling me that Jacob will be getting paid $448 a day?" Hannah asked Mike.

"Yes, and I will pay Jacob an extra $2 every day so he can make an even $450 every day. He will work Monday to Friday from 4:30 until 9:30," Mike said to Hannah, "Because I know that Jacob has school."

"Wow, that's $2,250 a week that Jacob will be making. That's almost twice what I make every two weeks. Let me talk to Jacob about it and we will call you. We just have a lot to go over first about his schooling and getting homework done every day before he goes to work for you. I am very big on education in my house."

17

"I hear you and I understand where you're coming from with that," Mike said to Hannah.

*****

The next day came and Jacob got ready for school with a smile on his face. He couldn't wait to share the good news with Corey and the rest of his friends.

"Yeah, I am about to get them new Jordan's within the next two weeks."

"Yo, what's up with me? You got me, bro?" Corey asked Jacob.

"You know I am going to bless you with a pair, brother. I never leave family out."

"Yes!" Corey shouted excitedly as he jumped in the air.

The little ladies in school all heard the news about Jacob and his new job he'd be starting on Monday.

"Hey, Jay," they said to him as he walked through the school hallways with a big smile on his face.

*****

Sunday came and Jacob could not wait to tell the people of God the good news about him starting his new job tomorrow. After he sang songs out to the Lord and praised with thanksgiving he was called up to the altar to give his testimony. Pastor Mark then brought forth the Word and preached a fire-landing message to the people of God, then church was dismissed.

Afterwards, Jacob and Hannah had some of their church family and Pastor Mark over their house for dinner. Hannah prepared a meal for everyone.

"I'd like to propose a toast to Jacob," Pastor Mark interrupted dinner to say. "May the Lord continue to bless you and keep you as you start your new job tomorrow. Remember to keep God first and He will direct your path with more blessings to come."

When dinner was over and everyone had left, Jacob and Hannah were washing the dishes.

"Jacob, I'm proud of you for starting work tomorrow. Just make sure your life maintains an order to it. God, family, school, and then work. Remain faithful to the Lord and continue to walk in the path that He wants you to walk in."

Jacob hugged Hannah with tears running down his face. "Yes mother, I understand." He said his prayers and went to sleep.

Jacob woke up the next morning to get himself ready for school. In math class his teacher asked a question and he raised his hand to answer it. He answered the question correctly and the teacher was very impressed. She asked him how he came up with the answer and after he explained to her how he did, she just looked at him in amazement.

After math, Jacob walked to his next period class and ran into his best friend Corey.

"What's good, my man? I see you will be going to work today after school," Corey said.

"Yeah today is the day when I start making that bread," Jacob replied.

"You got to look out for me and help me get a job at the shop."

"I will look out for you once I get my foot into the door but let me get in first," Jacob answered.

Jacob and Corey went to their next class, saw two of their beautiful young female classmates, and then started to joke around in class with them. While Jacob and Corey were in class joking around with the young women, the school fire alarm went off, most likely due to Zack, the school prankster, pulling the fire alarm to get out of school early. The two young women asked Jacob and Corey to come over one of their houses.

"Wait, we do not even know you so why would we go over your house?" Corey asked.

"To have fun," one of the girls responded. "We can show you a great time."

Jacob asked the two young women for their names. One of the young women stated her name was Latasha, and the other said her name was Lisa.

"Latasha and Lisa. That sounds like trouble," Corey said.

"Wow, L.L.," Jacob said with a laugh. "Well, I guess it won't hurt. We can chill with you two for the next three hours until the time that school really lets out. As long as I am at work around 4 o'clock," said Jacob.

"Wow Jacob, you have a real job?" Lisa asked.

"Yeah, today will be my first day. I will be cleaning up hair at the barber shop," Jacob replied.

Jacob and Corey left school with Latasha and Lisa. Lisa walked to the parking lot, pulled out her car key, and unlocked the door to a red drop top BMW.

"Wow," Corey and Jacob said in unison as they stared at the car.

"Lisa, you a baller," Jacob said. Lisa then batted her eyelashes and smiled. "My father is a lawyer and my mother is the director of First NA Financial Bank. My father has been working at the same law firm for over 22 years and my mother has been on her job for 24 years."

"Wow, that is great," Jacob said to Lisa, "I wish that I could have had my father around. You are lucky to have both parents, Lisa. All I got is my mother and we struggle because my mother has to work three jobs to take care of me. I am the only child so that makes things a little easier. My mom tells me all the time that my dad is looking out for me from heaven and we will always have help from the Lord to take care of us, which sometimes is very hard to believe."

"What happened to your father? Did he walk out on you and your mother?" Lisa asked as Corey and Latasha were having their own conversation in the back seat.

"My father died the day I was born," Jacob replied. "My mother was in labor with me and ready to deliver me. My father was on his way to the hospital to see me come to this world when he was killed in a tragic car accident."

"I am so sorry to hear that," said Lisa. "Now I can see why you're working to help take care of your mother."

Jacob looked Lisa directly in her eyes and said, "Yes, this is why I am working.

Lisa thought that was very sweet. She leaned over and gave Jacob a kiss. Meanwhile Corey and Latasha were in the back seat of the car making out. Lisa looked through her rear view mirror and screamed, "Slow down, hot tamales!" Everyone in the car laughed very hard as Lisa pulled up into the driveway of her house and then pressed a button in her BMW to open the gates to her mansion. Everyone in the car got out and walked inside.

"This is the life," Jacob said, giving Corey a high-five. They continued to walk around Lisa's house, stunned at all the fancy things her family owned.

"I can really get used to this," said Corey.

"If your boy plays his cards right you will be very used to it," Lisa replies.

"Really?" Jacob asked. "Girl, you funny. If we're going to have some fun then we need to start now because I have to be at work within the next four hours. Lisa, can you drive me straight to work when it's time?"

"Sure, Jacob," Lisa giggled. "Anything for you, boo."

"Oh, I'm your boo now?"

"I hope so," she responds, still giggling.

They walked to the second floor and into a big home movie theater.

"Wow, this is sick," Corey and Jacob said at the same time, high-fiving each other again.

"What movie would you people like to watch?" Lisa asked everyone.

"Let's watch *Fight to Live for Today*. This is a great movie I heard," said Jacob. "I've been wanting to see it. It's about this kid who is bullied but learns how to stand up for himself. It was directed by one of my favorite directors, Fred Rush. All his movies are very good and he is nominated for an Oscar."

They watched the movie and everyone loved it and could not stop talking about it. The time was around 2 o'clock and Lisa asked what everyone wanted to eat for lunch. Latasha decided to make cheeseburgers and fries with chocolate milkshakes for everyone. When everyone had finished eating lunch they went down the hallway and played laser tag for about an hour.

"This was very fun, Lisa, and thanks for opening your home up to me and my friend. I really hope I can come over sometime again," said Jacob. "Now the one last favor I need is for you to take me to work," Jacob reminded Lisa.

"I told you I got you, boo," she said. Everyone left Lisa's house and hopped back into her car to drive Jacob to work.

"What kind of work do your parents do, Latasha?" Corey asked her once they were settled into the back seat.

"They own several businesses downtown," Latasha replied.

"That's great," said Corey.

Chapter 3

TEEN LIFE

Jeremiah 29:11 KJV

For I know the thoughts that I think toward you, saith the LORD, thoughts of peace, and not of evil, to give you an expected end.

Lisa dropped Corey and Latasha off, and decided to spark up a nice conversation with Jacob to learn more about him. They each talked about themselves a bit and Jacob even asked Lisa questions about Latasha.

"Why do you want to know about Latasha's background?" Lisa asked. "Why do you care so much about her?"

"It's not like that. I just want to see what type of background she comes from if she is going to be dating my boy."

"Don't worry," Lisa assured him, "she comes from a family of money just like me and, in fact, she lives right around the corner from me."

"That is cool," Jacob said to Lisa as they continue to drive to Jacob's new job. Finally they arrive at the barber shop.

"Goodbye, Jacob," Lisa said, "I hope to see you again soon." She gave him a kiss.

"You will," Jacob stated before walking into the shop as Lisa pulled off.

As Jacob started to walk into the barber shop, Mike spotted him and began to speak to Jacob with a loud and mean tone in his voice.

"You are late on your first day," Mike said.

"I got into the shop at 4:01. My shift starts at 4:10."

"Never be late for anything that you do in life. Always be on time. It is better to be early than late. Being late leaves a bad impression of you. Do you understand me, Jacob?" Mike said to Jacob. Jacob replied with a yes.

Mike took Jacob down in the basement of the barber shop and introduced him to all the barbers. The people down in the basement were smoking marijuana and speaking with foul language that Jacob was not used to hearing.

"Tyree will get you up to speed on how to work here and what you will be doing," said Mike. Jacob went back upstairs with Tyree and then Tyree started to show Jacob what he would be doing and how to do the job.

26

"Hey, Jacob, please pay full attention to everything that I will be showing you today because this week is my last week here at the job. I am moving on to a new job and will not be around long to show you again," Tyree said as Jacob looked him in his face.

"Why are you leaving?" Jacob asked.

Tyree pulled Jacob into a quiet back area of the shop to speak with him privately. "It's way too much going on in this barber shop and when everything hits the fan I do not want to be around when it happens. That is all I'm going to tell you." Jacob and Tyree heard someone coming but when they looked to see who it was, the person had already left the area. It seemed like someone had been sneakily listening to what Tyree was telling Jacob. Tyree gave Jacob some basic training, and then Jacob started to work on his own for the rest of the day.

After a while, Jacob went on a quick 15-minute break but his break was interrupted when he heard Mike screaming from the top of his lungs at another man. He looked and then suddenly a gun appeared from Mike's waist and was raised up to strike the man right across the top of his head. Jacob could see the blood running down the man's face.

"Now this is the last time you are going to come up short with my money!" Mike yelled at the man.

"Yes! Please, I will have your money, I promise you!" the man replied fearfully. Mike told his goons to clean the man up and get the blood off the floor of his barber shop. As the goons grabbed the man Jacob stood, shocked at what he had just seen. Mike looked up at him.

"Are you hungry, little homie?" Mike asked him. "Man, I am hungry!" Mike screamed out loud. "Tracey, order some food," he demanded a woman who also worked in the shop. Forty-five minutes later the food arrived and everyone started to eat.

When it was around 9:30 PM Jacob got on the phone and called his mother to come pick him up from work. Twenty minutes later Hannah came into the shop to pick Jacob up, spoke to everyone in the shop, and left with her son.

"I know that chick from somewhere," Mike said to himself under his breath, "She looks very familiar." He grabbed his face with a curious look.

Driving home, Hannah noticed her son's silence and asked him if everything was okay. "Yes, everything is okay," Jacob said in a low voice.

"Okay, are you sure? Because you are not seeming like yourself."

Jacob changed the subject by beginning to tell his mother about his new girlfriend Lisa to take his mind off of what he had seen happen at work today. Jacob knew that if he told his mom what had happened at the barber shop she would stop him from working there and would not ever allow him to step foot in there again.

"So how long have you been hanging out with this Lisa girl?" Hannah asked Jacob.

"I just hooked up with her today and Corey is seeing her best friend, Latasha. Don't you think that is very cool? Two couples who are best friends on both sides? You see Corey and I plus Lisa and Latasha."

"I get it, son," Hannah replied back to Jacob. You just met her today, my boy," she said and smacked him softly on the back of his head teasingly. They both started to laugh and joke as they pulled up to their house.

"Do not worry, Mom, I will not do anything out the order of God," Jacob tells his mother.

"That's all I wanted to hear you say, son," Hannah said. "The Bible tells us how we should stay clean and pure until marriage. We cannot leave any room for the enemy to come into our lives, and me and your father are a full testimony of how to keep yourself until marriage. We did not have sex until we were both married to each other and we never had sex before we got married."

"Wow, that's very hard to believe."

"Nothing is too hard for God."

Jacob could not wait until he got into the house to call Lisa on the phone and speak with her about his first day of work.

"I could not wait to speak with you and hear your voice," he told her once she had answered the phone.

"I was thinking about you all day," said Lisa to Jacob.

"It has only been four hours since we saw each other, Lisa, come on," Jacob replied, laughing. A voice could be heard in Lisa's background.

"Yes, Mother?" she yelled aloud back to her mother.

"Come pick up the phone in your room. It's Latasha on the line," her mother said.

Lisa told Jacob she would call him back in 15 minutes after she spoke with Latasha.

"Hey, girl. What's up? Tell me all the details about Corey and you had better not hold anything back," Lisa said.

Latasha giggled. "We were talking on the phone for about two hours. I am finding out a lot about Corey and he is very smooth and charming," she replied, still giggling.

"Well, it's nice that you're getting a chance to know Corey but I wish I could say the same about Jacob. We have not had much time to talk because he was working and he just got home so we're going to have to catch up tomorrow in class, girl," Lisa replied to Latasha.

"Okay, goodnight. I will see you tomorrow in class," she said before hanging up the phone.

Lisa called Jacob back and he started telling her about work and the bad things he had seen at work, but that he didn't want to quit because he needed the job.

"Hey, you do not need to work at that job anymore if you don't want to. I have enough money to take care of us both," Lisa said.

"Yeah right, Lisa. You're still living with your parents and we are both young teens. We cannot get a house, lines of credit, or anything without getting it in our parents' names. If you think your allowance that you saved up is enough for taking care of us both then you've got to be one crazy chick," Jacob replied to Lisa.

"Hey, that is not nice, and for your information, I got about $10,000 saved up."

"Holy sweet heaven! You mean to tell me you have been saving that much allowance that your parents give you? That is a lot of money, Lisa, and you can make many good moves with that type of bread. But I am okay. I'd rather for you to keep your money because at the end of the day you took your time and saved it. I will get my money up like that by working, and besides, the Bible says if a man does not work a man does not eat."

"Alright, Pastor Jacob. You love quoting scriptures out the Bible. I noticed that about you. Some day you will be a preacher that will speak the Gospel of Jesus Christ. I can already see it," Lisa said to Jacob, laughing.

"That is what my mother says, what the pastor of my church says, and what my friends and family say. Do you know Jesus was preaching the Gospel at the age of twelve?" Jacob asked Lisa.

"No, I did not know that. Wow, and see how you know about the Bible and the history behind it. I always wished I knew the Bible more."

"You can, Lisa, and to do that you just have to study the Bible by showing you are self-proving unto God. You have to spend time praying and asking God to show you things and to guide you into more truth because this is a crazy world that we are living in today."

"You are so right and maybe this is the reason why you are in my life."

"Well okay, it was nice talking to you but I think it's time for me to get to bed and get ready for school tomorrow, God willing, because if my mom comes in my room and hears me still on the phone with you at 11:45 PM on a school night she will flip. Before we go to bed let us say a quick prayer," Jacob said to Lisa. "God, in the name of Jesus, please watch over us as we sleep. Help us study your Word more and let us put you first in everything we do. Protect us from danger and anything that is not like you. In the name of Jesus, we know that you put us here on this earth to do your work and move by your will. Help us not to think about ourselves and learn to help others.

Forgive us for any sins that we might have done or things we may have said or done that are not righteous to you. Help us understand this world, as it is very difficult to be young teens growing up. And if you see my dad tell him I love him. In Jesus' name, Amen."

"Wow, that was a great prayer, Jacob. How did you learn to pray like that?" asked Lisa.

"I learned by watching my mom and as I got older I just started to have conversations with God as if he was standing right here in my room."

Hannah had been listening to Jacob's whole conversation with Lisa. She knew that it was a little past 12:00 AM but she did not go into Jacob's room and say anything. She just walked away from his room door and started to thank the Lord for what she could see in her son's life. She went to her bedroom and sent a powerful prayer up to heaven. Jacob and Lisa wrapped their conversation up, told each other goodnight and then went to bed so they could be ready for school in the next seven hours.

*****

It was 8 o'clock on Tuesday morning and the bell rang as all the kids were walking to their classes. Jacob looked up and saw Corey getting into an altercation with some kid. They were about to fistfight until Jacob got in between them both to break it up.

"Stay out of this, Bible boy," the kid said to Jacob, pushing him. "This is between your boy and me. He was walking with my girl and I do not play that!"

Latasha was coming down the hallway. "I am not your girl no more, boy, bye! You had your chance a long time ago. I am feeling Corey now. He is way more charming than you and knows how to treat a woman," Latasha said.

In a flash the boy had reached his hand out and smacked Latasha to her knees. She was now bleeding and started to throw punches. Soon Lisa, Corey, and Jacob jumped in, and as Jacob turned around he was met with a fist in his face as one of the kid's friend got into the fight to help his friend. The fight went on for about 25 minutes with no security guards or teachers coming to break it up. Finally, the NTA security guards came and the fight was broken up.

A fight that started with two people ended up having about 12 people sitting in the principal's office. After everyone was questioned about the big altercation, Jacob, Corey, Lisa, and Latasha sat in the office cracking up laughing, talking to each other about how wild and crazy the fight was. As the principal sent them to their classes, Lisa asked if everyone was down to hang out at her house again after school. Everyone replied with a yes, and Jacob said, "Yeah, I am down but I can only stay for an hour. I have to go to work."

Chapter 4

TEEN PEER PRESSURE

Proverbs 13:20 KJV

He that walketh with wise [men] shall be wise: but a companion of fools shall be destroyed.

It was Jacob's 18th birthday and he was celebrating with family and friends. Lisa and Jacob had been dating for a while now and Hannah had been all over his back about getting married. Jacob explained to his mother in private that he and Lisa had not been sexually active with one another and not to worry. As Jacob started to open gifts from family and friends, the doorbell rang. Corey answered the door and Mike walked inside the house.

"Jacob, my man, happy birthday, little homie," Mike said.

"Thanks, man," Jacob replied.

"Why don't you go look outside," said Mike.

Everyone followed Jacob outside, where he found a black AMG 63 Mercedes-Benz. "This car is sick, Mike! When you get this car, man?" Jacob asked Mike.

35

"Just yesterday," Mike replied, throwing Jacob the car keys. "Go take it for a ride. Happy birthday, li'l homie. Enjoy your new car."

"Wait, you mean to tell me that this car is my new ride, Mike?!" Jacob said. "Thank you, Jesus! This is sweet. God is so good," Jacob said. Everyone just stood in shock, looking at Jacob's new car. As Mike walked over to say hello to Hannah, Pastor Mark arrived and saw Mike at the house.

"Mike, what is good and what are you doing in this house? This house is holy ground," Pastor Mark said to Mike.

"Hey, man, I just came by to bless Jacob with his new birthday gift because I knew you could not afford to get him a new car like the one you see parked outside the house."

Pastor Mark laughed. "Mike, I know Jacob works for you but that will soon change. Do yourself a favor…stay away from this house and never come around here. As I told you, this house is holy grounds of God."

"What if I don't?"

"Just wait and see if you think this a game because you and I both know God is greater than you."

"Ha-ha! You are a funny man, Pastor Mark. You really think God is the answer and that He will really save you. If this is the case why is he not saving your behind?

You keep on praying and praying for God to perform a miracle in your life and nothing is happening for you yet. Your church is about to be foreclosed on and it isn't no money coming into the church because people do not really believe in that crap you be preaching. How are you going to preach the Gospel and have the people believe what you preach about when you can't even get the repairs done at your church? You are broke, preacher. That is in the way of life. Instead of being in the church, you could be out here in these streets taking over, getting money with me, and living the good life. We used to be best friends and bang together hand to hand. The old you was a gangster; not a preacher and you had it all, but you threw it away just to preach the Gospel," Mike said boldly.

"Look here, Mike, you lame dude, you are only up for a season. Don't you know sin is only for a season and if you do not turn to the face of God, your days on this earth will be numbered? In the Bible, Matthew 4:4 tells us, *Man shall not live by bread alone, but by every word that proceedeth out the mouth of God.* Therefore, I'd rather stand in on the Word of God than live a luxury life and die in hell. I'd rather live my life poor and make it into the kingdom of heaven than live rich and wake up in hell being tormented by the devil and his demons. We both did things we're not proud of and God gave us second chances and helped us move forward in life. Why throw all that away? We both have children and will be held accountable for all the things we do in life. Remember, Mike, it does not matter how big we get; just know that God is bigger and greater. He made this world for us, so everything in the world will come to me if I continue to trust in His Word.

Men and women lie all the time but God does not lie. I know things look bad for me now but God will work it out for me because I walk by faith and not by sight."

Mike looked at Pastor Mark with hatred in his eyes and said, "Whatever, weirdo."

"You can say whatever you want but just remember what I said. Do not come around this house anymore because you and I both know this is not the place. I know your every move and see everything you do because I used to be you; let us not forget. God used Jacob Sr. to lead me to the light and get out from darkness. It's my job to look out for Hannah and watch over Jacob Jr. God rest Jacob Sr.'s soul while he is with the Lord, but he showed me how to live righteously and how to walk in the path of Jesus Christ, the living God, and keep walking to the finish. I want to see my grandmother and my parents along with Jacob Sr., but for me to do that I must continue to walk in the path of the Lord; not your path," Pastor Mark said to Mike.

"Go ahead with all that church talk," Mike said, walking away.

Pastor Mark just laughed, shaking his head as he thanked the Lord and walked over to Hannah and Jacob.

"Daddy, Daddy!" Latasha said as she arrived at Jacob and Hannah's house, running over to give Mike a big hug.

"How is Daddy's favorite girl doing today?" Mike asked her. Latasha threw a punch at Mike and hit him on his arm. "You're starting to be very heavy handed. Are you still hitting the heavy bag I got you for Christmas last year?"

"Yes, Daddy," Latasha replied to Mike.

Jacob stood, stunned at finding out that Mike was Latasha's father.

"Is everything okay with you, Jacob?" Lisa asked.

"Hey, Latasha, let me holla at you real quick," Jacob said to Latasha.

"Sure, what is it?"

"So is Mike your real dad, Latasha?"

"Yes, Jacob. What, you did not know Mike was my dad? Corey never told you?"

"No, he never told me at all and we've been dating you two for a while now. Wow," said Jacob. "It is cool. I will talk to Corey when we get the time to talk. It's just that it is a small world to be so connected."

"I see my dad got you a nice new car. It would be nice if he could grab me one as well."

"I am just as surprised as you, Latasha," Jacob said.

"I know you know all about my dad's business now after working at the barber shop for so long and you know it's just a front cover for what he really does. Let us just keep all the stuff he really does between us and do not tell anyone. I know you see many crazy things that happen with my dad while working in the shop."

"Yes, I do and it is not pretty. There are some crazy things that go on in the shop. You would not believe half of it if I told you."

"Oh, I believe you and I bet it is scary," Latasha said to Jacob.

"Let's cut this cake so we can go out and have a good time. It's Friday," said Jacob.

Everyone wished Jacob a happy birthday and Hannah said a quick prayer for her son, thanking God for keeping him this far as he was becoming a young man. Jacob cut the cake, thanked everyone for the gifts, and served the slices of cake.

A whole hour went by and people were starting to leave the house. Lisa came up with the idea for the rest of the crew to head to her house as both of her parents would be out of town for the next four days.

"Hey, Lisa, ride with Latasha. I am going to ride with Corey. We got a lot to talk about and it's a nice little ride to your crib anyway," said Jacob.

"Oh, is everything okay with you two?" Lisa asked.

"Uh, yeah," Jacob replied back to her. Lisa and Latasha got into Lisa's car, and Latasha left her car parked in Jacob's driveway. Corey looks into Jacob's eyes and could see that he was not happy at all, as they got into Jacob's new Mercedes-Benz.

"Hey bro, all this time you knew Mike was Latasha's dad?" Jacob asked once they had pulled off.

"Yeah, and so? What is your point, Jacob? I been working for Mike myself for a while now," Corey said to Jacob.

"What you mean you been working for Mike yourself? And what kind of work you been doing, bro? Because there's only one job I know that you're doing, and that's in the barber shop. Give me a straight answer, no lies."

"Alright, Jacob, you want to know? I am a delivery boy for Mike. I deliver a black duffle bag back and forth from a warehouse to Latasha's house four times a day."

"What?! Are you crazy? Do you even know what is in that black bag that you carry around? You carrying drugs, Corey, and we cannot play with that. You are on dangerous grounds carrying that type of work with you. All it takes is for you to be pulled over by the police or either robbed for the whole bag and it is a wrap. You will be in hot water! I don't even want to speak about what Mike will do to you if that bag were ever to go missing. Do you really think Mike will give you a pass because you are dating his little girl? He will kill you for his bread, and

FREDERICK B. RUSH JR.

between you and me, I have seen him do it many times over the past few years I have been working for him. Did you know that he was Pastor Mark's right-hand man and they both used to run the streets together until they were raided by the feds? Pastor Mark did not tell on Mike. Instead, he took the heat and did two to five but was released in a year for good behavior."

"No, I did not know all that, Jacob, but all I wanted was to make money like you. After you looked out and got me the job at the barber shop, it opened doors for me to work on other opportunities. It seems to me that you are mad because Mike promoted me and not you."

"Are you serious right now, Corey? I know you just did not say that to me because right now you are sounding like a dumb nut. If you think giving you a black bag to deliver back and forth four times a day is a promotion then you are crazy. If you get robbed or caught with all that work, it's going to be your problem, Corey; not Mike's. If it was like that why did he buy me the $95,000 brand new black AMG 63 Mercedes-Benz?"

"Come on, bro, did you have to rub it in my face?"

"No, I am not saying it to rub it in your face. I just had to let you know not to think highly of yourself. The Word of God tells us all that we should not ever think highly of ourselves or we will fall. I could have had that job but I knew that it was not honest and within the next few months I am quitting this job if I get accepted to Christ United Nations University."

"Yeah, I heard of that school. It is a Christian college, right?"

"Yeah. So before you start doing things for Mike make sure you really do your homework on him. He is a good person but he's still heavy in these streets and I learned in the past to stay out of his way seeing what type of moves he makes. He is no one whose bad side you want to get on. So be the smart friend that I know you are and tell Mike you cannot deliver his goods for him anymore and he has to find someone else to do that for him. That dude is going to go down and I darn sure am not trying to be one to go down with him. Mike is headed down the road of destruction," Jacob said to Corey as they pulled up in Lisa's driveway.

"Man, I am going to bang Latasha's back out," Corey said to Jacob.

Jacob looked at his friend with sadness and disappointment. "What is wrong with you, bro? What has gotten into you?"

"It's not about what's gotten in to me; it's about who I've gotten into," Corey said with giggles, "Don't tell me that you have not tapped Lisa yet. Man, I done already started tapping Latasha about four months ago," Corey said to Jacob.

"That's crazy, bro. I am going to pray for you guys because you know the order of God; no sex until you get married and you should have saved yourself until the day you and her say I do."

"Come on, Jacob, you mean to tell me that you did not tap Lisa yet?"

"No, I have not and will not until we both say I do on our wedding day. I got my father and God looking down on me and I made a promise to my mom and God that I was going to wait. I do not have to have sex to show Lisa a good time, said Jacob to Corey."

"Okay, so you mean to tell me that Lisa is going to sit and continue to wait around for you to give it up when she got so many dudes on her top? Come on, man, we seniors and we go off to college next year. Do you really want to graduate school as a virgin? Man, you are tripping. I am telling you this because it is a fact that if you do not tap Lisa she is going to move on. She already told Latasha that if you two do not do it before school lets out it is over between the two of you. Look, bro, I am only telling you this because you put in so much time with this girl. How will you feel if all of sudden someone else scoops up your chick? Tonight is the night. You can go in this crib, take Lisa upstairs in her room, and tap that like a homerun in the ninth inning."

As Corey sat, telling Jacob what to do, Jacob sat there looking at Corey with a curious look, thinking about what his friend was saying to him. He did have a point, in a way. Then Jacob heard the Holy Spirit of the living God speak out very boldly and bluntly to him. *"Jacob, this is not the way. Your way is never the way I have planned for you. Remember to continue to trust in me and not the way of the world for the wages of sin is death as I told you in my Word. Continue to follow the footsteps of your father as he*

44

walked a righteous life up until his death and just wait for the day you enter these gates."

"Jacob! Jacob! Jacob!" Corey called his name three times to get Jacob's attention.

"Oh, my bad, bro. I was just listening to what God was saying to me," Jacob replied.

They walked up to Lisa's door and rang the doorbell. Lisa invited the fellas into the house by telling them that the door was unlocked. As they walked into the house Latasha grabbed Corey and started kissing him and making out with him. Meanwhile, Jacob heard Lisa call him from upstairs. He could hear her voice but could not make out where she was. Finally, she told Jacob to come inside the movie theater where they always hung out. As Jacob went inside the room he saw Lisa sitting on the top of one of the chairs wearing a hot pink lingerie set with hot pink heels. Jacob stood shocked with his eyes and mouth opened wide. Lisa grabbed him and started to kiss him, and he was breathing very loudly and heavily. Jacob then started to shake as Lisa sat on his lap and began to give him a lap dance to a song that she'd turned on.

"Lisa, why you are doing this to me?" Jacob asked her.

"Because I want to give it to you," she replied and then continued to kiss him.

"Oh Lord," Jacob said as they got deeper into making out. Lisa reached into the pocket on the chair and pulled out a condom.

"Here, put this on," she said, handing it to him.

He shook his head in refusal but then he began to think about what Corey had said to him in the car and what God had told him in the car as well. As Jacob was thinking, Lisa distracted him from his thoughts. She started to lick his ear and caress his body in all types of places where a young man would like to be touched by a young woman. Jacob grabbed Lisa and started kissing her back roughly. He started licking her all over; on her back, her chest, and her legs. Lisa took Jacob by his hand and led him into her bedroom where they began having heavy sex. The sex was great for the both them; so good that the room started to spin in a 360-degree motion because it was the first time that either of them had sex.

They had sex for about an hour and then got dressed and walked downstairs to the kitchen to get something to eat. They were laughing and sharing food with one another. Then Corey and Latasha came into the kitchen and they all started a conversation about graduation and the colleges they all were waiting to hear from. Lisa started to show off for Latasha by kissing Jacob right in front of her and Corey.

"Yeah, that's my boy! That is what I like to see," Corey said to Jacob as Jacob looked back with a smile on his face.

"Hey, I will be right back," Jacob said before taking off to the bathroom. After using the bathroom Jacob looked into the mirror and could not even recognize himself anymore. It was like the light of holiness was removed from him and the connection between him and the Lord was lost.

Jacob laughed to his reflection, saying to himself, "I feel great." He was happy that he was no longer a virgin. Little did he know he had just opened the door for the enemy to come into his life and his family's life. The curse would soon rain upon him, as God was very disappointed in him. Jacob then hopped into the shower, washed himself up, and then got dressed again. He then walked back downstairs.

"It is time for me to bounce because I have to be at the shop for work in the morning," he said.

Lisa looked at Jacob with sad puppy dog eyes. "Can't you two just stick around for a movie and then leave?"

"I am down with that," Corey said, "What about you, Jacob?"

"I guess I can hang for another two hours and watch a quick flick."

"Latasha reached in her pocket and pulled out two blunts already rolled up. Everyone started smoking and the room soon became clouded with the heavy smoke.

After two hours had gone by everyone was so high they felt that they were through the roof. "Hey, Jacob, we out. Let me hold the keys so I can drive. I want to see how this new car rides," Corey said. They gave Lisa and Latasha kisses goodnight and then started to drive home. "My mom may be over your house anyway so I am going to crash at your crib," Corey said to Jacob.

"Sure, no problem, bro. It's all good," said Jacob, giggling, "I know our moms are up talking about what they're going to do when we get into the crib." As they walked into the house they could see the looks on their mothers' faces. Hannah, Carla, and Jackie were up late watching the Praise Network having church in the house.

"Jacob, do you know what time it is?" Hannah asked her son.

"I know you know what time it is," Corey's mom, Jackie, said.

"Yeah, it is 2 AM. What's your point?"
Jackie grabbed the broom from the kitchen, swinging it at him and yelling.

"You better get upstairs, boy! Trying to get me out my spirit."

"We got a lot to talk about in the morning before you get to work, son," Hannah told Jacob.

*****

48

The next morning Hannah knocked on Jacob's bedroom door and gave him a long lecture about him staying out too late and how he had to do better. But Jacob was not really trying to hear that because it was the same stuff his mom always talked about to him, so it went in one ear and out the other ear.

"Yes, Mother," he said once she had stopped talking. Jacob woke Corey up and they both ate breakfast, got dressed, and then drove to the barber shop. When they arrived they saw police tape and bullet holes everywhere. The doors and windows were all shattered.

"What happened here?" Jacob asked a police officer that was on the scene.

"There was a major shootout here about 35 minutes ago and we are investigating," the officer told Jacob. "Do you young men work at this shop?"

"No, we don't," Corey replied back to the officer as Jacob looked at Corey angrily for lying to the police officer. Corey got a phone call from Mike, telling him and Jacob to meet him at the diner that he always took them both to.

FREDERICK B. RUSH JR.

Chapter 5

A YOUNG ADULT WITH A HEART OF GOLD

Jeremiah 1:7 KJV

But the Lord said unto me, Say not, I am a child: for thou shalt go to all that I shall send thee, and whatsoever I command thee thou shalt speak.

As Jacob and Corey arrived at the diner they saw Mike sitting with a tall cup of coffee. He was on the phone talking about how the barber shop had just been hit and how he planned on making the next move on the guys who put in the work. Jacob and Corey sat down with Mike and he began to tell the two of them how everything went down.

"Hey, man, what the heck happened, though?" Jacob asked Mike.

"Man, we been infiltrated. This happened early in the morning when I was opening up the barber shop. All of a sudden I saw a black car ride down the block and they started shooting at me. I ran off the step and into the alley behind a small car as shots continued to rain down around me. Then just when I thought everything was over I went back out and I saw a big SUV come down the block

51

shooting at me with more shots," said Mike. "I was strapped too so I pulled out my 40 and started clapping back. Then one of my mans came up the street and he started clapping at the SUV too. The cars sped off and the next thing you know we heard police coming so we bounced from the scene. My man went his way and told me he would get at me in an hour, and I drove straight here where I know I am safe and clear away from the law."

Mike's phone started to ring. It was his boy on the line. Mike's eyes grew very wide as if he had gotten some very bad news. He had found out that a person named Big Rome who he thought he had killed over six years ago was, in fact, not dead and was the one who put the hit out on him. "Oh, it is on now. It's about to be a war!" said Mike. "Corey, did you drop that bag off where I told you to?"

"Yeah, I did but why was this bag more heavy than the other bags?" Corey asked with a curious look.

"Those were guns in there this time. I was selling them but now that we're at war I need them back."

"Isn't there another way out of this, other than going to war?" Jacob asked.

"No, li'l homie. Them dudes shot my barber shop up so now they have to pay and it is as simple as that. Let me ask you something, Jacob, are you ready to bust your gun?" Mike asked.

"No, the only gun I am busting is for Jesus," said Jacob.

"I knew you were not ready, but Corey, you ready, right?" Corey looked at Mike with a crazy look.

"Hey, Mike, we love you like a big brother and all but we're not cut from the same cloth you cut from. You have this type street stuff built in you and really don't care," Jacob said to Mike. As Mike was listening to what Jacob was saying he got a note from one of the waiters with a message saying *Mike, you have not seen anything yet. Leave town now because you are never going to be safe.* Mike balled the note up and set it on the table as he shook his head.

"This is getting crazy. We have to shut Big Rome down," said Mike.

"No disrespect, Mike, but *you* got to shut Big Rome down because I am not trying to get myself involved with this type of heat. I can clearly see this is not a game and I can't play with this man. These type of acts will put me six feet under or in jail for life and I am not trying to take a life because I have a lot I'm looking to do with my life," Jacob said to Mike.

"Look here, li'l homies, y'all both already involved. The very moment I gave the both of you jobs working for me you became involved. When I am at war then you both are at war as well because Big Rome does not care who he hits when he blazing them shots. Seven years ago he killed a little 5-year-old girl in crossfire, shooting at me," said Mike.

Corey and Jacob looked at one another with shocked looks on their faces. Corey burst out into tears. "Man, that was my little sister who was killed in that crossfire!"

Jacob tried to calm Corey down. "I know what you're thinking but this is not the way to go, bro.

Mike looked at Corey with a grin. "This is an opportunity to get even and set the record straight with these clowns. So what do you say, li'l homie? You gonna ride out in this war with me?"

Corey nodded his head. "Yes, I am down. Count me in."

"This is not the way, bro," Jacob said. *"Vengeance is mine,* said the Lord."

"Look, right about now I do not want to hear none of that Bible talk from you Jacob because where was God when my little sister was killed? Did God think about saving her then? Now I got the drop and I am going to make it hot for this Big Rome cat. You always talk about how people should be baptized in the Holy Spirit. Well guess what, my G? These nines is going to be baptized when they done clapping at this Big Rome cat!" Corey said.

"Yeah, that's what I am talking about," said Mike. "These dudes going to know that this is our town and this time I will make sure that a bullet goes right inside his wig so I know Big Rome is dead for sure."

"With the wages of sin is death; remember that Corey," Jacob said as they were leaving the diner.

"Whatever, Jacob. As I said, I am not trying to hear all that Bible talk. It is on and my mind is made up."

As the three of them continued to walk, a black undercover police car pulled up in front of them and two officers jumped out and grabbed Mike. "We need you to come down to the station because we have a few questions to ask you about what went down at your barber shop," one of the officers said, grabbing him. "I know you know what happened so hop in this car and take this ride with us."

"Come on, man, this is crazy. I do not know what happened because I was not there," Mike said to the police.

"Then if you were not there you should not have a problem coming down to the police station. Just come and answer our questions, then you can be on your way."

"Hey, li'l homies, I will hit you two up as soon as I am done talking to these pigs," Mike told them.

"You better watch your mouth because you're about to be in our house and we can make moves on you so play nice, boy."

"Yeah, whatever. Let's just get this crap over with because at the end of the day you're wasting your time," Mike said to the officers. "Corey, do not tell Latasha about this. Keep it low because I will not be able to hear the last of this if the wife finds out. Listen out for your phone just in case they try not to let me go for any reason."

"Alright, no problem, Mike. I got you. Say less," Corey said.

Jacob looked at Corey. "Man, I know you are much smarter than this. You do not even know or realize what you are about to get yourself into. Let me ask you something, are you trying to impress Mike because you are dating his daughter?"

"Naw man, it is not even like that but that does help because Mike will know that I am the man for his little girl. But the truth is that people change as they get older. I am not the same kid who always went to church and to Sunday school because back then I had no choice, but now I am becoming a grown man and making decisions for myself instead of always letting my mom decide what I need to do," Corey said to Jacob.

"You can still make decisions, Corey, but just make good ones and not ones you make just because you think they are going to make you look good and impress other people. Now this war that is about to go down with Mike and Big Rome, you are not built for this type of drama. I know it and I know deep down in your heart you do not really want to do this, man" said Jacob.

"Naw, bro, you wrong. Them dudes killed Christina and they have to pay for that. She would have been about to turn 13 in two months if she was alive today and I always made a promise that if I found out who did that to my sister that I was going to handle them. I am in this Jacob with or without you. I just hope that you can ride with me on this one," said Corey.

"Man, do you think it is that easy to take someone else's life?"

"No, but I guess that I will find out when I clap this burner at them fools. I need to know if you're down or not within the next two days, bro, because I plan to ride out real soon."

"Yeah, you right. But before I see death Big Rome is going to see death first; believe that."

*****

Meanwhile, back at the police station Mike was being questioned very hard and the officers were trying to put the pressure on him by telling him that he better give them something or he will be looking at some time.

"You whack cops do not have anything on me. I been down this road a few times and if you had something on me I would have been locked up by now. I told you what I knew and that is it. I am the one that is a victim in this. My shop was shot up all crazy. Why are you not trying to find the people who did it?" Mike asked.

"Well, this is why we are asking you, because we would like to be of good service to you," said one of the police officers to Mike.

"I will let you guys know if anything comes up," Mike said with a smile on his face, knowing that they'd have no choice but to let him go. Finally, the cops put Mike back in the same car and dropped him off where they had picked him up.

*****

As Jacob and Corey sat in Jacob's house telling Hannah everything that had gone down, Hannah cried with a heavy heart. She started to pray aloud with her hands laid on Jacob and Corey.

"Corey, I need you to trust and believe in God because this time the enemy is really riding your back and wants you to fall into a full path of destruction. He wants to see you play his hand but you have to continue the will of God. Just think about how you found your little sister's killer out of nowhere after seven years. This is clearly a trick of the enemy, who wants to set you up to take your life and stop you from going into greatness. You have your life ahead of you and you can accomplish great things. Do not throw it away to get revenge for your sister. Be better than that and leave it in the hands of the Lord. I am sorry and cannot forget about Christina, and rest her soul, she is with our Lord, but she would not want you to get into this," Hannah said to Corey.

The doorbell rang and it was Lisa and Latasha.

"Why haven't you picked up your phone or responded to any of my text messages?" Lisa asked Jacob as she and Latasha walked into the house.

"I know Corey knows what is going on!" Latasha yelled. Corey looked at Jacob and shook his head.

"Today was a crazy day, babe," Corey said.

"Have either of you spoken to my dad today? Because his phone keeps going to voice mail," said Latasha.

"We were with him a few hours ago at the diner eating but he left us and we have not seen him since then."

"So what is this I'm hearing about my dad's barber shop being shot up? I am going to ask again, what is going on? And is there something that either of you want to tell me?" Latasha asked Corey and Jacob.

"Let them know what is going on because you owe them that since you two went half the day not answering your phones," Hannah told them.

"Okay," Corey said, "but when I tell you this do not say anything. Your dad is down at the police station getting questioned about the shooting that went down at his barber shop and a dude named Big Rome, who your dad thought he killed back in the day, is still alive and getting back at your dad. Here is where it gets crazy; remember when I told you about my little sister Christina, who was killed in the crossfire of a shooting seven years ago?"

"Yeah, I remember," Latasha replied.

"Well the shooting with your dad and Big Rome killed my little sister."

"Oh, no." Latasha started to break down crying and fell on the couch.

"Mom, there is something more to this," Jacob told Hannah.

"What else, Jacob?" Hannah asked with a small tear in her eye.

"Pastor Mark was one of the men shooting at Big Rome. He was working with Mike back when they used to be best friends. Now that Pastor Mark has turned his life around, he's been preaching the Gospel of Jesus. He has left the street life and does not have a clue that Big Rome is alive," said Jacob, filling Hannah in with the missing pieces.

"So let me get this right, Jacob," Lisa said, "You are saying the preacher who stopped by at your birthday party was best friends with Latasha's dad?"

"Yes, Lisa, that is exactly what I am saying."

"No disrespect to you, Latasha, and I know you know what type of life your dad is into, but Mike and Pastor Mark were best friends, and Pastor Mark did a few years. Pastor Mark turned his life around for the good while your dad continues to live the same life he'd been living," said Jacob.

"One is a gangster, and one is a preacher now. Wow, that is crazy," said Corey.

"Mom, you have to call Pastor Mark and speak with him to give him the heads up about Big Rome because if Big Rome sees Pastor Mark he will try his best to kill him. They thought that they killed Big Rome and Pastor Mark was involved just as well as Mike was, so Big Rome does not care; he is going to let his gun cough. There's about to be a very big war and the streets are about to get crazy so we have to brace ourselves for what is about to happen," said Jacob.

"Yeah, you're right, and Latasha, we got to keep you safe because if Big Rome finds out that you are Mike's daughter he will try to take you out as well," said Hannah. "Hey, why don't you ladies go home and get some sleep? The boys will not be able to hang out with you tonight because we have a few things we need to discuss."

"Okay, no problem. Goodnight," said Lisa as her and Latasha left the house. Lisa and Latasha got into Lisa's car and drove off.

After they'd been driving for about 15 minutes they noticed a black Cadillac with black tinted windows following them on the road. They turned off to go in a different direction to see if they were being followed, and sure enough the car turned also. Lisa hit the gas and drove hard, going 85 MPH on the road. The Cadillac following them sped up also. As both cars drove fast, out of nowhere red and blue police lights started blinking and the cops pulled over the Cadillac.

"Oh, thank you, God. That was very close," Lisa said to Latasha.

"Hey, did you see the front plate that was on the car, Lisa?" Latasha asked.

"No, what did it say?"

"It said Rome Associates."

"So what do you think?"

"I think it was some of Big Rome's goons trying to get us tonight but thank God for the blood," said Lisa.

"Hey, shut up with all that Bible talk. You've been hanging around Jacob too long. No one is trying to hear that talk right about now. Just get me home," Latasha said to Lisa.

"Whatever. You are really your father's daughter," Lisa said.

Chapter 6

UPCOMING PREACHER ON THE RISE

Jeremiah 3:15 KJV

And I will give you pastors according to mine heart, which shall feed you with knowledge and understanding.

Lisa dropped Latasha off at her house but as she was leaving to head home she noticed another car hanging around. She soon realized it was only some neighbors. Finally, Lisa got home and called Jacob to tell him about her and Latasha being followed and how the car was pulled over by police.

"Wow, this is crazy. We have to do something quick because it is starting to not feel safe," said Jacob. "I have to study these scriptures for Sunday service because Pastor Mark asked me to bring the Word Sunday for Youth Week."

"That is great Jacob! So when were you going to tell me?" said Lisa.

"Hello! I am telling you now, duh, but I had to get your news first," Jacob replied.

"Don't *duh* me. I was just making sure that you were telling me first, that's all," Lisa replied to Jacob.

"I talked to Pastor Mark and he is aware of Big Rome's return after seven years, so he is on the lookout," Jacob told Lisa.

"How did Pastor Mark know about Big Rome? Who told him? Your mom?" Lisa asked him.

"I do not know because Pastor Mark would not tell me. He just said that his ear is still to these streets even after becoming a pastor."

As the night ended so did Jacob and Lisa's conversation. The next day came and the phone rang at Hannah and Jacob's house.

"Hey son, the phone. It's Corey on the line," Hannah told Jacob. He picks up the phone to talk to Corey and Corey tells him the story about Lisa and Latasha being followed the previous night.

"Yeah bro, I already heard the news and it is getting crazy. I do not need this type of heat right now because I need to get ready to preach this Sunday," said Jacob.

"So what you trying to do today? Chill at Lisa's house?" Corey asked.

"No, I am starting to get tired of chilling over there. Let's go to the mall and spend a little money because I need to get fresh for Sunday. Plus, I need some new wardrobe anyway," said Jacob.

"Yeah, I feel you bro. I am in need of some new wardrobe myself because lately my swag feeling as if it is below zero," said Corey.

"Okay, that sounds like a plan. I am going to hit Lisa and ask if they want to come along and then hit the shower up and I will be by your house in the next two hours."

"Cool, I will hit Latasha's phone and ask her too. See you in two. Peace."

"Jacob did you pray when you woke up this morning before you thought about talking on the phone and calling Lisa about going to the mall?" Hannah asked her son.

"Yes Mom, I did. I don't even know why you would ask me a question like that. You know I will give the Lord thanks before doing anything."

"Okay, I am just checking."

Jacob spoke to Lisa about going to the mall and she told him that it sounded good to her and that Corey and Latasha were both down with going too. Jacob got dressed, then rode to Corey's house and picked him up. On the way to the mall, Corey's cell phone rang, and it was Mike on the other end of the phone asking Corey to go pick up a new bag from his Mexican friend on 28th Street. Corey informed Mike that he would and that he was on his way.

"Yo bro, what did we already talk about before about this delivery stuff for Mike? Why can't you just listen and chill with this before you get yourself caught up real crazy?" Jacob said to Corey with an angry look.

"Look bro, I hear you but I still work for Mike and need to keep getting this money because it's very easy money and comes fast. Plus Mike looks out and gives me a bonus on my pay for looking out for him," Corey replied. "You have to understand it is easy for you to say. You already riding nice and your chick riding nice plus Latasha. I am the only one that is not riding clean. My car keeps breaking down. You got a car handed to you that you did not even have to work to get."

"So then ask yourself Corey, after doing all these deliveries and pickups Mike never gave you a new car, right? I never had to do any of the type of work that you did and still got a brand new car. You would think that it would be the other way around and that you would have the new car and not me. This should tell you right now that Mike is using you bro," said Jacob. Corey just looked at Jacob, realizing that he was right.

"Corey I love you and you my brother but after this last pick up and drop off we cannot do this anymore because this is crazy and I cannot get caught up just because you wanted to keep being a wannabe drug dealer," said Jacob.

"Man, how you going to sit here and say something like that to me? We like brothers. We playing on the same basketball team and shared animal crackers together, right?" Corey asked Jacob. "Hey bro, I know it sounds a little shady for me to be saying this to you but this is what you are when you keep doing these pickups and drop-offs for Mike. You are a drug dealer even though you're only transporting. You may not be putting the drugs in smokers' hands but you might as well be doing that too. Do you think if we are pulled over by the police that they want to hear that it is not yours? They will ask you that and if you say no they will ask you who it is for and then they will try to make you snitch and say a name. You and I both know what happens to the people who break the no snitching code," said Jacob to Corey.

"Okay Jacob, you right. So now let us just get the stuff and keep it pushing," said Corey. Jacob's cell phone rang and it was Lisa asking where they were and saying that she and Latasha were already at the mall waiting on them. Jacob let Lisa know that he and Corey would be at the mall in 15 or 20 more minutes.

Finally, Jacob pulled up to Corey's destination and Corey stepped out and grabbed a big black bag from Mike's Mexican friend. As Jacob and Corey drove off Mike called Corey to confirm his pickup and Corey let him know that he got the bag and asked where it needed to be dropped off. Mike told Corey to take the bag over to Light-skinned Chris' house and leave it there with him. As Jacob drove he started wondering and becoming curious about what the drugs looked like in the big black bag so he pulled the car over and popped the trunk open. Corey stepped out first and ran to the back of the car and Jacob came right behind him. They opened the trunk and Corey opened the bag up and saw that in it was nothing but guns.

"See bro, this is what I am talking about. This is crazy. It is five years for each burner that we got in this car right now. Hold up, let me count how many there are." Corey looked at Jacob like he was crazy as Jacob counted the guns. "Man, I cannot believe this is 43 burners."

"No, it's 44. Here's one that slipped out into your trunk," said Corey as they both shook their heads while putting everything back. Jacob then found a few business cards on the side of the big black bag that belonged to the same Mexican guy that sold Mike the guns. Surge West was the name on the card along with his phone number.

Jacob and Corey hopped back in the car to drop off the guns to Light-skinned Chris' house, which was on the way to the mall. After driving for about ten minutes out of nowhere a police car rode up next to them, making Jacob nervous. The police car was not thinking about them at all until Jacob's anxiety caused him to run the red light. The police car turned on its lights and pulled behind them to pull them over. Jacob knew that if they were pulled over with 44 guns it would be over and jail time would be coming. Jacob's life flashed before his eyes as he thought about facing a judge in court. He knew there was only one way out even though he really did not want to do it.

"I am not going to jail today," Jacob said aloud as he put the pedal to the metal and sped off down the highway.

"Man, what is you doing?!" Corey asked Jacob.

"Put your seatbelt on and be quiet, man," Jacob said with aggravation and anger all over his face. Jacob cut into the right lane, hit the brake, then cut into the left lane, sped up, and then made a quick left off the highway. He rode past the park then cut into a tunnel off 13th and Jones Street and as the police sirens began to fade away Jacob cut down a small street and backed the car into a small alleyway. He got out the car and started screaming at Corey.

"Get these burners out my trunk and take them to Light-skinned Chris now and never ask me to drive with nothing in my car from Mike again! This is crazy. Today you and me could have been in jail because of this dude. If you want to be Mike's robot then you will do it by yourself!" said Jacob to Corey. Corey grabbed the big black bag of guns, walked about four houses down the alley way, and knocked on Light-skinned Chris' door. Chris answered the door and Corey handed him the guns.

"Yeah man, it's good. I just got off the phone with Mike. Thanks and stay up li'l homie," said Light-skinned Chris.

As Corey got back into Jacob's car he looked at Jacob and saw the look on his face. "Hey man, I am sorry and you know what, you are right. Today my life flashed in front of my eyes. I saw myself being in jail for another grown man. If Mike wants stuff picked up and dropped off he has to do it himself. I will no longer be putting in this type of work," said Corey.

"Thank you, man. This is the smartest thing I have heard you say in the last two years. Stop doing Mike's dirty work and let him handle his own business because all he's doing is using you to save himself a trip to jail. If you keep doing his work, you are going to be taking his place in one of two ways, and that is either dead or in jail," said Jacob.

"You are right again, bro, but now that we've been to hell and back let us get to this mall to meet with those chicks," said Corey.

"Oh, you have not been to hell yet but if you keep hanging around and doing Mike's work, you will see hell fast," said Jacob as he laughed at Corey.

Finally, Jacob and Corey showed up and caught up with Lisa and Latasha at the mall and started shopping.

"Hey, remember I have to get me a nice suit to preach my sermon this Youth Sunday," said Jacob.

"Babe, I think you would look nice with a black shirt and a nice blazer over it," said Lisa.

"Yeah Jacob, Lisa is right. If you're going to be bringing the Word this Sunday you have to switch your swagger up a little better," said Corey.

"Look, I do not need to swag myself out just to bring the Word to the people. I am doing this for the Lord and not to impress people. They need to hear that Jesus died to save them so they could live. As long as my message gets to them I've done my part. It is not about dressing; it is about being a blessing," said Jacob.

"That was hot Jacob. Not about dressing but being a blessing. You would do well as a rapper if you ever decided to be one," said Latasha as she repeated Jacob's lines.

"Hey babe, I understand what you're saying but just think, you will have people coming from off the streets this Sunday so if you switch the swagger up a little it will help the youth relate to you more rather than them just seeing you in the suit," said Lisa.

"Okay babe, since you know best you can pick out my whole outfit for Sunday," said Jacob.

"Wow, really? That's what's up. Then let's hit these stores up now," said Lisa.

Everyone was shopping in the mall, spending money like there was no tomorrow. They each left the mall with a bunch of bags, including Jacob's bag from Luke's Suits. Jacob grabbed a gray blazer, a black button down shirt, and black jeans with gray prints, along with a pair of black suede Bruce shoes. Now all Jacob needed was a cross chain to wear while he preached.

As everyone was leaving the mall, they saw a big guy walking with four to five people around him. He was wearing all black with a chain that said "Big Rome." He had a big hole on the left side of his face with a long scar across his head as if he'd had brain surgery. As he walked by, he looked at the four of them and asked if there was a problem.

"No, there's not a problem unless you want to make a problem," Corey said, looking at Big Rome

"What, li'l man? Do you know who I am?"

"No."

Big Rome snapped his fingers and two of the guys with him started walking over to the four of them, but the mall security rushed over between the two groups and called the police. Big Rome and his goons left the mall quickly as they did not want any trouble with the law.

"Man, that was another stupid move you made again," Jacob yelled at Corey.

"Look man, I am not going to let another grown man talk to me like I am some punk in front of my girl and I don't care who it is. If you want to be scared that's on you. I was talking fly because Big Rome is not dumb; he will not try anything with people around to witness it," said Corey.

"Man, do you wake up in the morning and pray to ask that God give you wisdom because that's what you need to do. What happens if he sees you on the streets somewhere, genius? What will you do then? I am your bro and down for you and would have no choice but to help you ride on this fool if he tried to come back at you. I am always in mess because of something you're doing and I do not ask for it, but somehow and some way it comes my way from you," Jacob said to Corey angrily.

"Hey babe, I hear what you're saying but you need to be easy on Corey," said Lisa.

"Mind your business, Lisa. This is between A, my man, and B, me, not you, so C your way out of this," Jacob said to Lisa.

"Oh, I know you're not talking to me like that, you jerk. You had better watch the way to talk to me. I am not Corey. This is me you're talking to," said Lisa to Jacob.

"Well you're saying be easy on him but you would not be saying that if you heard what this man put me through," said Jacob.

"What he put you through?" she asked him.

"This man is doing drops for your pops, Latasha."

"What?" Latasha responded with a surprised look on her face.

"Yes, this man picks up and drops off for your dad. It's drugs and sometimes money."

"What the heck, Corey? Is all this true? Is this what you've really been doing when you tell me you are dropping off? When I asked you told me that is was pizza you were delivering to try to buy a new car but the whole time you were lying to me," said Latasha.

"Hey, here is where it gets worse. Today we picked up a big black bag of guns for your pops, Latasha," said Jacob. "Yeah, that's right, guns. And then we had to take them to Light-skinned Chris on the north side and were chased by the police on our way there."

"The police? What is this, Corey and what are you doing? This is not how we roll," said Lisa.

"Exactly. So from now on do not sit here and tell me to take it easy on him because I'd rather talk to him and let him know than see Corey dead or locked up," said Jacob to Lisa.

"I did not know my dad was really into this type of stuff at all. This is all starting to be very scary to me and I do not know what to do," said Latasha.

"Don't worry, we are all here for you and will be by your side as we figure it out. Just do not let your dad know that you know these things about him," said Lisa.

"I am sorry, y'all, and I am going to do better. I do understand what I get you into Jacob and it's my bad, bro," said Corey.

"It's cool, Corey. Just do not let the trick of the enemy pull you in and use you for bait," said Jacob. Everyone got ready to leave the mall because it was closing in 15 minutes. Lisa asked Jacob to ride with her and Jacob gave Corey his keys to drive with Latasha to Lisa's house.

As both cars were driving on the highway, they saw fire trucks driving very fast down the road, and as they neared Lisa's house they saw that it was her house that was on fire.

"What?! Oh no, oh no, Lord. Please don't let this be," said Lisa as everyone got out the car and ran to Lisa's house. There was thick smoke but they could see that only a small part of the house was on fire. The firefighters put the fire out quickly and then one of them came to speak with Lisa.

"Is this your house, ma'am?" the firefighter asked.

"Yes," Lisa replied.

"You are truly blessed not to have this house burned down in flames. Who lives here other then you?"

"My father and mother and our housemaid, sir," Lisa replied. "I forgot that I left the house without taking the chicken out of the oven. I got so busy with other things that I forgot to turn the oven off and take out the chicken. I really want to thank you for getting here so quickly because my parents both are out of town for business. I do not know what to do. I want to get the house repaired before my parents come back home," said Lisa.

"Hey, I know of someone that may be able to do the repairs for you within 48 hours but he will be very expensive," Jacob told Lisa and then made a phone call to one of his church brothers. Jacob then confirmed the time with Lisa for his church brother to come out and begin the repairs on the house.

The next morning Jacob's church brother came to Lisa's house and started to repair the part of the house that was damaged in the fire. Lisa got a phone call from her parents saying that they would be home in the morning and she started going crazy. She needed at least 48 hours to get the repairs done. She begged the repair guy to please try to have the work done by that night and even offered him more money to hire some help. He hired a few more men to help him and they worked hard and fast.

Finally, all the repairs were done and everyone left except the one brother who stayed to add the final touches to the job. Jacob and Corey pulled up to the house with Chinese food to chill with Lisa and Latasha. Everyone went into the movie theater down the hall from Lisa's room. As everyone ate, talked, and watched the movie Lisa whispered into Jacob's ear and told him to come to her room. She said she had something she wanted to show him.

"Hey babe, shut the door and close your eyes; no peeking," said Lisa to Jacob. Jacob closed his eyes and told her to let him know when he could open them. Finally

Lisa told him to open his eyes and when he did he saw her standing there in a two-piece light blue lingerie set. Lisa was licking her lips and shaking her hips as she started to make her way over to Jacob. Like last time, the Holy Spirit began to speak to him, telling him to resist temptation and avoid fornicating. This time Jacob allowed the Holy Spirit to speak to him and he listened. He tried his hardest and focused on the words he was hearing instead of the sight of Lisa in front of him. He quickly fled the room to avoid committing the sin. Jacob ran back into the movie theater with Corey and Latasha and saw that they were both naked and kissing. As Jacob headed downstairs, he heard Lisa yelling after him. "Jacob, where are you going? Get back here!," said Lisa, while following him to the front door and out of the house. "Why are you leaving in the middle of the action?," she asked.

"So you were about to give me the booty action huh?" Jacob asked Lisa, smirking at her and shaking his head. "I have a sermon that I have to preach to the youth tomorrow morning in church. How can I ever expect to preach or teach if I am doing everything that compromises the Word of God? I have to learn how to live a holy life if I want to preach the Gospel of Jesus Christ like my father used to. It is time to stop playing church and live a godly life. This world is really coming to an end and I need to be ready. I will not lose my chance to get into the kingdom of God," he said boldly to Lisa.

"Hey babe, I understand that you are being real serious with God and I will not get in the way of that. I have needs and I want what I want, but if you're not willing to give me what I want then it may be time to move on," said Lisa.

"Hey, I will not stop you because if you're going to break up with me because I do not want to have sex with you then our love is not real; it is based on sex. I love you Lisa but I love God more than you and I hope you can really understand that. If not, then cool, maybe you're not really the one for me and God got someone else for me. But really I would love to get married and for you to be my wife," said Jacob.

"Wow, really? That would be great because we've been together for some time now," said Lisa.

"Let's just keep ourselves from this day forward and allow God to bless us to be married, and then we can have all the sex we want with each other and we will not be convicted when we do," Jacob replied. "Look, it is getting late and I have to bring the Word tomorrow so I am going home to pray and study some more. Have a good night and I will see you in church tomorrow if God wills for us to see tomorrow." Jacob ended his night by kissing Lisa on the lips and then drove off to head home.

As Jacob was driving on the road to go home he stopped at a red light and a car pulled alongside of him, rolled down the window, and put a gun out the window. Jacob was praying and asking for protection from the Lord when out nowhere, a loud laugh came. The window rolled down a little more and Jacob looked up to see that it was Mike.

"Come on, man, why you playing with me like that?" Jacob asked Mike with a frustrated look on his face.

"Come on li'l homie, you should have seen the look on your face. You were shook and looked like you was ready to pee your pants. It was just a little joke. I did not mean to hit you with a heart attack," said Mike, laughing uncontrollably.

"Whatever, man. Grow up and stop playing all the time. You know like I know Big Rome is on your head and I think he knows who I am because we saw him in the mall today."

"We need to link up at the diner on Monday. I have some things to talk to you about. I know tomorrow is Sunday and you are gonna be doing you so just get at me Monday. Peace," Mike said as he drove off.

Jacob finally got home to pray and study the Word some more and then he went to sleep. The next morning Hannah knocked on his room door. "Jacob, get up. It is time to get ready for church."

"Okay, Mom, I am getting ready now. I'm about to get into the shower." Jacob showered and put on all the new clothes that Lisa helped him pick out at the mall and went downstairs.

"Whoa, look at my son looking sharp and like a million bucks!" said Hannah proudly.

FREDERICK B. RUSH JR.

"Mom, you shot out and so crazy but I'm glad you like what I got on. I will drive today," Jacob said. As they drove to church, they saw Pastor Mark and he waited for Jacob and Hannah while Jacob parked the car in the youth pastor parking spot. Pastor Mark walked Jacob and Hannah into the back of the church through the pastor's entrance. Jacob prayed unto God for him to bring the Word to the youth and as he was praying he heard a song from the praise and worship team. Jacob cried out to the Lord as he fell on his knees and started to thank Him. He was very happy and felt extremely blessed to be bringing forth the Word from the Lord; this had been one of his prayers for the past two years and he was finally getting the chance to preach a message to the youth.

Pastor Mark came out to greet the congregation and welcomed them to Youth Sunday. He thanked everyone for coming out and prayed that the message Jacob brought forth would have people leaving as changed individuals and that they would not leave church today the same as they came.

"Please welcome Jacob," said Pastor Mark as he walked Jacob out on the pulpit.

"Good morning, church, and praise the Lord," Jacob began. "I said praise the Lord everyone! We need to give thanks to the Lord, as He is worthy to be praised." The congregation was getting hype, thanking the Lord and screaming and shouting His praise. "I want to open my sermon up with a prayer because it is not about me, it is all about Him, the Lord. Dear father, in the name of Jesus, I thank you for today. I thank you for the lives that you will

80

change today. You said in your Word that you are a man that would not lie. If I ask I shall receive and I ask that I can help change people's lives today. Put anything that's not like you to the side and I ask that you cancel any work of the enemy and that you bring back your people to the love they need to have for you. In Jesus' name I pray. Amen," Jacob prayed.

"If you have your Bibles with you today I would like you to turn to 1 Corinthians 13:11, and the Word reads: *When I was a child, I spake as a child, I understood as a child, I thought as a child: but when I became a man, I put away childish things.* Today we run around as grown men and women acting like little kids. We can even act younger than our children can today. It is time for us to throw away the kids' stuff and bring out the grown stuff," Jacob said, waving his Bible to the congregation. "The other day I saw a sister from this church going into the club and she is about maybe 35. I asked myself why she is going to a club at 35? It is over for that. If you did not do that already then you need to chill. You know who you are, my sister, and I am not going to put you on blast because I am not God, but just know that I will be praying that you line your life up with Him more. I am not any better than anyone is here in this church. I sin sometimes and fall short of the glory of God, for the Bible says we all sin. We have to know when and how to turn away from sin. Do you know that one of the reasons God had to form as a man using the body of Jesus is that he could not look at sin? Adam sinned as a man and caused corruption to this earth so God had to form himself as man to fix what Adam jacked up. He had to become the last Adam to save the world. Jesus died on the cross and took a beating for us to live again by shedding his blood on that cross. We do not have the time to be playing church!" Jacob yelled out to the congregation with boldness. "We have to throw away childish things and start doing grown things. Start by living a godly life to set an example for other people that are not living right. Can I get an amen, church? The Lord is still working on us but it is our job to meet him halfway. Hallelujah!"

When Jacob finished preaching the Word he called a few people up to the altar to pray for them. Jacob noticed Mike sitting in the back of the church with four goons. As Jacob prayed for the last person, Mike got up and left the church with his four goons, and Corey darted out of the church after him.

"Wait for me. I'm coming too," Jacob could hear Corey saying as he followed behind Mike and his men. After descending from the pulpit, Jacob went over to Lisa and Latasha and saw that Latasha was crying.

"Hey Latasha, what's wrong? Why are you crying?" Jacob asked.

"I overheard my dad sitting in the back of the church talking about he had to come today to ask the Lord to forgive him for what he was about to do," said Latasha.

"What is it that he's about to do?" Jacob asked her.

"He's gathering all his goons to go to war with Big Rome." Jacob said a quick prayer with Latasha and asked God to give her peace about what was about to go down.

Lisa asked Jacob and Latasha if they wanted to go out to eat after hearing Jacob's powerful sermon. As they were leaving the church, Pastor Mark called Jacob to speak to him. "Hey, God bless you, my brother. You did a great job today preaching the Word. To God we give the glory. Listen Jacob, please do not hang out with Mike or get caught up with the drama he is in right now. The Lord is trying to help you grow into the new path of becoming an up and coming preacher on the rise, and you have to stay into the Word because God is about to do some good things in your life. You cannot allow the enemy to get in the way of you doing the work of the Lord. I know about Big Rome and if he steps foot in this church he will give his life to Jesus Christ. I know I did many bad things but old things pass away and I am a new creature in Christ. We have to throw away the childish things, as you preached in your sermon today," said Pastor Mark to Jacob.

Everyone left the church and Pastor Mark locked up. Jacob, Lisa, and Latasha drove to a restaurant where they had dinner and a long talk about the Word Jacob spoke from the Lord that day.

FREDERICK B. RUSH JR.

Chapter 7

THE COLD HEART OF A MAN

Matthew 5:8 KJV

Blessed are the pure in heart: for they shall see God.

As Corey met up with Mike, they began to load up the guns and strap up as if they were ready to go to war with another country. Back at Rome's Palace, Big Rome and his goons were loading up their guns and getting ready for war as well.

"Hey, the first move we got to make is getting at that cat Mark. He thinks because he is a preacher that his life is going to be cool. Preachers can get a wig shot too and I still haven't forgot about him leaving me for dead. So now it's time. Dude got to pay," said Big Rome to his goons. "As for that dude Mike, I wish I could kill him first, but I know his life is like mine and it's going to be a little harder to take him out. All I know is that cat Mike is going to wish he was dead because I am going to kill him slow."

"But Big Rome, why kill the preacher? He is out the way now and living a Godly life. He changed his life around for the good and is no longer in the streets," said Rick, the head of Big Rome's goons.

"Look, I do not care if Mark is a preacher now or not. He wasn't a preacher when he left me for dead alongside of his right-hand man, Mike. Now it's time that he pays for his sins because God forgives but I don't!" said Big Rome as he laughed.

As the day turned to night, Big Rome and his goons started to move out. They made their first stop at Pastor Mark's church and one man went around the back of the church and snipped the wires of the alarm system to stop it from triggering. A few of Big Rome's goons made their way inside the church and started trashing the place. They broke some of the chairs in the church sanctuary and knocked many big holes in the walls. They even spray painted some of the walls and the church media sound booth. They broke windows and doors, making the entire church look like an abandoned building. Finally, Big Rome and his goons left the church and moved out.

A few hours later Jacob, Lisa, and Latasha left the restaurant. As they rode by the church they saw Pastor Mark along with Hannah speaking with the police. You could see the tears running down Hannah's face as she cried out, "Oh God, why would they do this to the house of God?" Jacob immediately ran to Hannah to comfort his mom and held her in a big hug. Pastor Mark had an angry look on his face as if he wanted to get back at the people who did this to his church, his place of worship. Jacob, Lisa, and Latasha went into the church and saw how bad the church looked after being trashed. Spray painted on the wall next to the pulpit were the words **Jesus cannot save**

you, Pastor Mark, because you are still a dead man walking.

As Pastor Mark stepped into the church with Hannah he spoke to Jacob, Lisa, Latasha and the rest of the other people that were inside the church. He explained the situation to everyone with tears in his eyes and said he knew the people who were responsible for it. "It takes a man with a cold heart to do something like this to a place where people worship. Lord, please forgive me, as I am for wanting to turn to my old ways right now."

"Hey, Pastor, let us get everyone together so that we can pray. We have to trust and believe that God will work a miracle for the church," said Hannah. Pastor Mark grabbed the hands of the people of God and said a super prayer. They worshipped for about an hour and then everyone started working on the church and doing small repairs.

"Hey, has anyone heard from Corey?" Hannah asked Jacob, Lisa, and Latasha.

"Corey is with my dad and his goons ready to bring on a war, Ms. Hannah," said Latasha.

"What? A war? All this will do is cause more chaos and bring more pain to people and their families. I pray and hope Corey can use the wisdom of God and snap out of it to get his mind right because it is a trick of the devil to trap him and kill him in a sin," said Hannah. "Hey, Jacob, did you at least try to talk to Corey before he left, because I already knew about it. You guys talk about everything together," Hannah said to Jacob.

"Yes, Mother, I did and guess what? He did not want to hear anything I was saying to him because all he cared about in his mind was getting revenge for the death of his little sister Christina. I can tell Corey the way but cannot hold his hand because he is a grown man and able to make decisions on this own. It is all up to him whether he chooses right or wrong and I cannot make him choose the right way. He knows that only he can do for himself," sighed Jacob.

"Hey, son, you know what? You are correct and I am sorry if I may have been a little hard speaking to you on Corey but let us pray that he returns," Hannah said.

The people inside the church said another prayer for Corey per Hannah's request. "It is clear that the church and some of God's people are under attack by the enemy. It's time that we all put on the armor of God and the helmet of salvation with the Word of God as the sword to fight the devil and his demons," said Pastor Mark.

As everyone left the church and went home for the night Mike and Corey were with all Mike's goons, ready to move out for the war. Big Rome and his people had already moved out and were on the way to Mike and his crew. Little did Big Rome know, Mike already had the drop on him and had a man set up inside Big Rome's crew as a driver. The driver took Big Rome and his goons to a dark, wide street. Big Rome looked at the street and saw that it looked very familiar, but he could not fully put two and two together. It was the same street that he was left for dead on seven years ago.

A black SUV spun fast down the street and four men hopped out and started clapping shots at Big Rome and his crew. Big Rome reached in the back of his truck and pulled out a sawed off double barrel shotgun and started going to work with it, blazing back at Mike's goons. The way Big Rome was moving while operating the shotgun you would have thought that he was much younger and in better shape than he was.

Mike pulled up with Corey and two other people in his car and Corey rolled out then ran behind a trash dumpster and started shooting at Big Rome and his goons. Corey had two 9mm pistols in his hands and was just running around crazy, busting shots everywhere. One of Big Rome's people crept up behind Corey and was about to do him in. Mike was right behind Corey backing him up and he shot the guy right in the side of the neck with his 40 caliber with its thin rubber grip. Rome saw Mike and Mike saw Rome, and they started to exchange words as they were blazing theirs guns at each other.

"Not this time, G. I told you that it was on this time and you should've killed me while you had the chance!" Big Rome yelled at Mike.

"Well, this time I am going to do you so dirty that you are going to wish I'd really killed you the last time," Mike replied as they continued to fire shots at each other, both missing every single shot.

As shots from all angles continued to rain down, bodies were falling and more goons were coming from both sides. All at once everyone heard police sirens approaching.

"Hey, Mike, come on man. Get in the car!" Corey screams to Mike. Big Rome had already run out of shotgun shells and Mike took advantage of that and caught Big Rome with a single shot in the arm. Big Rome hopped in his car, screaming in pain.

"Yo, drive this car!"

"Yeah, your boy Joe set us up, man," one of Big Rome's goons said to him as the car pulled off. "Did you know that he was working for Mike the whole time?"

"So Joe lined us up by driving us to this location? Okay, I got something for this dude. Wait until we get back to the spot. I got him," said Big Rome.

As police cars arrived on the scene, Mike was back at the spot with the team collecting all guns from the goons. He then gave them to a gun stasher to hide so there would be no guns if the police decide to stop by and do a search.

"Hey, everyone, good work out there. I know we lost Ziggy and Slim K, but we will make sure that we take care of their families with all funeral arrangements. They were like family and will be truly missed, but remember that is the game. We will lose many people when we at war, and it is far from over," said Mike to his people. Corey sat quietly with a sad look on his face. He knew he had gotten himself into something that he may not get out of easily. Corey's phone started to ring. The caller ID showed that it was Latasha on the line trying to check on him but instead of answering his phone he pressed the ignore button on her.

90

"Alright, people, I will holla at y'all later," said Corey to Mike and the team.

"Alright, li'l homie, I will holla at you in the morning to go over our next move," said Mike to Corey. Corey got in his car, lit his blunt up and started smoking his weed. He drove to a quiet place to relax and clear his head after the work he'd put in with Mike and the rest of the team. Meanwhile, Latasha was starting to worry about Corey because she'd been calling him and had not been getting an answer from him. She came to Jacob and asked for prayer because at this time she needs a Word from God to help her feel better. Jacob started to pray with Latasha and speak life over his friend in hopes that he would return.

Corey finally returned home to see Latasha waiting on his front steps outside of his house. She spoke her mind and let him know that she was not feeling what he was doing. Corey told Latasha of the experience he'd had going to war with her dad and the rest of his team against Big Rome and his crew.

"Corey, you're not a gangster so why are you trying to be one?" Latasha asked him.

"I feel I am starting to turn into one and now is the time I get revenge on Big Rome for killing my little sister seven years ago. It does not take a gangster to bust your gun at these fools these days. I am a young boy that is going to gain respect," said Corey.

91

"What do you really have to prove to people, Corey? When you live by the gun, you die by the gun and you already know that, so you had better stop doing what my dad tells you to and follow your own mind," said Latasha.

*****

Meanwhile, at Jacob's house, he and his mother were discussing how much the church repairs would cost and how to get them done. "Pastor Mark will be taking up special collections on Sunday," said Hannah. Lisa said that she told her parents what had happened and they were willing to help get the church repaired. "Praise God!" Hannah yelled out. "That will be great." Everyone said goodnight to each other and as Lisa drove home Jacob and his mother went to sleep.

The next morning came and everyone got dressed and rode down to the church to start working on the repairs. Lisa and her dad came to the church and spoke with Pastor Mark, then cut him a nice check to pay for all the repairs needed at the church.

"I do not know how to tell you how grateful I am for donation you gave to the house of God. May He truly bless you for this. I just wanted to tell you how much of a great man and father Lisa has in her life," Pastor Mark said to Lisa's father.

*****

After many days and many hours of work in the church, it was finally repaired and better than ever before. But as Pastor Mark stepped outside he heard someone speak out to him.

"What up, Mark? What, you thought I was dead? Look again." A black car with tinted windows pulled up and Pastor Mark could see that it was Big Rome. Pastor Mark looked at Big Rome as if he was a ghost coming back from the dead. As the car drove off Big Rome screamed out to Pastor Mark, "Yeah I'm the one who trashed the church and I am going to do it again, but this time I will burn it to the ground."

"God is greater, Rome, and you are small in the Lord's eyes but I will pray for you," Pastor Mark yells back before Big Rome turned the corner of the block.

*****

Two days later, Sunday service started and Pastor Mark shared his testimony with the congregation about how God had blessed the church with the repairs. He called Lisa's parents up to the front of the church to thank them for donating to the church. Pastor Mark then went on to preach a powerful and touching message and then called for a board meeting. He talked about hiring security at the church and explained that Big Rome was out there and trying to kill him for something that was done seven years ago. He also explained how he did not want to put anyone from the church in any danger, so hiring security would be best until Big Rome either came to Jesus, lost his life, or went to prison. As Pastor Mark spoke, he brought up

93

Jacob's graduation and how he would like to have the church help raise money for Jacob to go off to Bible College; to get him ready to learn more about the Word of God and move into his calling of becoming a pastor soon.

"So Hannah, how much money do you have saved up already for Jacob to go off to college?" Pastor Mark asked.

"Well, Pastor, as of today I have $72,000 saved up. Remember, I've been saving ever since Jacob Sr. was alive and I was only six months pregnant with Jacob Jr. We need to raise $18,000 more by August 15th to be able to pay the full $100,000 for him. The school will let Jacob attend for six years and he will earn his Master of Theology. The school only gives you the deal for $100,000 if you pay in full because the real price is $120,000. So you save $20,000 paying in full all up front," said Hannah to Pastor Mark.

"So how much time does he have to finish so he won't lose the money, since he may want to take a one-year break or a few extra months to finish?" Pastor Mark asked Hannah.

"The time is ten years on a six-year degree," Hannah replied to Pastor Mark. As Pastor Mark, Hannah, and the members of the church wrapped up their meeting they all agreed to donate money and everyone left the church to go their own separate ways. Pastor Mark locked up the church, set the alarm, and drove off from the church. As Pastor Mark was driving he looked to his left and saw Corey sitting on someone else's steps smoking a long joint.

Pastor Mark pulled his car over and told him to put the weed out and step into his car. Corey cried out for help from Pastor Mark and told him about the crazy shootout that he'd taken part in the other day with Mike and the rest of his goons. As Pastor Mark spoke to Corey, he let him know that Mike was using him for his dirty work and that he needed to really part ways from Mike because hanging with Mike was going to get him killed and or land him in jail. Corey let Pastor know that since he lost his little sister seven years ago he really didn't care about life. All his friends were going to college and he still had not heard back from any colleges yet.

"Keep applying, young brother and God will make a way for you because God is too good to let you be in these streets, but you have to meet him halfway. You have to really cut off all the negative things and involve yourself with positive things in life, like fully giving yourself to Jesus because He is the way and the light," explained Pastor Mark. Pastor Mark then laid hands on Corey and prayed for him to change his ways. Corey asked God for His forgiveness as he knew that he murdered at least two men during the shootout. As Pastor Mark continued to speak to Corey he let him know that he had to continue to pray to the Lord and ask him to keep him with a clean heart and not let him be walking around with a cold heart because it's the trick of the devil to take his life.

"Corey, do you know that the devil only wants to steal, kill, and destroy you? The devil will use you for a good season and then throw you away as if you are trash. The Bible tells us that sin is only for a season and this way we cannot fall into the devil's traps. We are in the last days and it's getting real out here in this world so this way we need to be armed with the power of Jesus," Pastor Mark said to Corey.

"Pastor Mark, do you own a gun for your protection?" Corey asked. "I figured you must have one being that you know Big Rome did not die when you and Mike ran down on him," said Corey.

"I do not need guns, Corey. Don't you know that I got the best gun you can have in life?! That's having the blood of Jesus and anyone or anything that is not Christ-like will go down because if God is for me who can be against me? My God can wipe out Mike and Big Rome and the good part about it is that I will not have to worry about going to jail for shooting either one of them suckers! Don't get me started on them because I will preach again after already coming from church preaching to the glory of God! Once you know, really know how good God really is you will not let small people like Mike and Big Rome get to you. I am walking in my own hood and not hiding and people know where I live, but guess what? They are scared to come my way because it's the Christ that's in me," Pastor Mark said.

Corey was amazed at the powerful words coming from Pastor Mark. He saw him as someone who really believed that he was invisible and started to think about what Pastor Mark was saying and thinking that he didn't need the guns. "Okay, Pastor Mark, enjoy the rest of your Sunday," Corey said.

"You do the same, young brother, and remember to just keep applying for them colleges and continue to pray and ask God to help you. Trust and believe in Him and He will direct your path. Then the next thing you know you will be in college. God Bless," said Pastor Mark.

Corey went straight home and jumped on the computer to apply for more colleges. Pastor Mark went home to relax and watch football because his team was in the playoffs. He was hoping they'd win and move to the next round.

*****

A few months had gone by and things had really calmed down with Mike and Big Rome's war since the police were looking for the both of them. Mike went on the run and temporarily moved to Miami with a fake ID under the name Melvin to keep a low profile. Using his new name, he was still able to move around and make his money out on the streets. Meanwhile, Big Rome was hiding out and staying at his sister's house in Mexico. He knew he was safe from the police there.

Pastor Mark and Hannah started getting closer to each other as Pastor Mark had always had a crush on her, but out of respect for Jacob Sr. he didn't feel comfortable enough to try to be with her. So he had to continue to pray and ask God to show him the right way. He thought that maybe Jacob Sr. would have wanted him to take care of his wife since he was no longer on this earth.

Jacob, Corey, Lisa, and Latasha were getting everything prepared for their graduation with things like their caps and gowns, school class pictures, and the best part—their school senior prom.

"Hey, man, I'm going to look fly for the prom," stated Corey.

"I hope you're not spending your money crazy, bro, because you don't have a job anymore since the feds raided and took the shop," replied Jacob.

"Yeah, of course I do. I got a lot of money, man, for real," Corey said, laughing.

"What do you mean? For real? How much money, Corey?"

"Remember the old closet in the barbershop basement with the real ugly mirror on the door that we did not like?"

"Yeah, I remember. What about that closet, Corey?"

"There was about $65,000 in a box with a lot of old books covering the money," said Corey.

"What? That's crazy. Do you know what Mike will do to you if he finds out that you got his money? He will cut your fingers off one by one and feed them to his dogs. When will you learn, Corey? It is always something new with you, bro, and you always getting into a mess.

Right now things are normal. No blood on the streets and even better, no crime. You and I both know that Mike is only a few hours away and he checks on Latasha every now and then. You about to cause something else because you took something that does not belong to you," Jacob said.

"Look, man, Mike is on the run and as far as he knows the feds got the money, so as long as no one starts talking then everything is cool. I am trying to go to school because it is crazy. All of you got the money to go. I do not. I am not trying to be stuck around the way while you all enjoying college and having all the fun without me. Mr. Holy, if you would have seen the money you would have took it too because I know you."

"If you think I would've then you do not know me after all, and the sad thing is we've been friends since we were four years old."

"Hey, come on. You two stop this going back and forth and let's focus on the things we need to do because my dad does not know about the money and if he did he would have already asked about it," said Latasha.

"Let's just all go to the arcade and play some video games because none of you can beat me in 21 Black Ninjas," Lisa said.

"Yeah, I am not going to lie Lisa, you are the best in that game. There was a time Jacob was the best until he started teaching you how to play," said Corey.

"It's only a matter of time until I get the crown back, babe, so hold on to it as long as you can," Jacob said to Lisa. Everyone headed to the mall and they all went on a big shopping spree and bought their wardrobe for the senior prom, which was only two days away. After shopping they went to eat at a nice restaurant. Jacob had the orange chicken pizza while Lisa ordered the crispy jerk lamb and Swiss cheese sandwich. Corey had his lobster cheese steak on a toasted long roll, while Latasha ate the ruby salmon and goat cheese sandwich. Everyone was very happy with their food and after they finished they had dessert and went home to go to bed and get ready for school. Everyone was also happy that they only had a few days of school left, and could not wait to have their summer break before heading to college.

The next morning as Jacob and Corey were at their lockers talking about the basketball game that had aired last night someone from the school office came to Corey and handed him a letter that said to call home ASAP. Corey ran to the office with Jacob and called home. When Corey called his house his eyes got very wide and he started screaming, "Thank you, Jesus! You are awesome!"

"What is it, bro? Tell me. Tell me, what is it?" Jacob asked as Corey looked at him with tears of joy in his eyes.

"Bro, I was just accepted to TM School of Music, which was the first school I applied for. Praise the name of Jesus, bro!" Jacob and Corey hugged and danced unto the Lord.

The two ran to Lisa and Latasha and let them know the news. "Wow, that is great!" they both replied and then everyone went to class.

*****

The next day had finally come and everyone was getting ready for the prom. Corey was over Jacob's house getting dressed. Latasha was over Lisa's house getting dressed. Jacob and Corey headed to Lisa's house with Corey driving a rented gray phantom ghost. Hannah and Pastor Mark were there while the photographer took pictures of them all before they left for the prom. Tears ran down all four of their parents' faces as they sat back thinking about their kids when they were just babies.

"Hey, you people have a good time, be on your best behavior, and remember no hanky-panky stuff," Hannah told them.

"Okay, Mom, go in the house!" Jacob shouted to Hannah as Corey kissed Latasha.

"Hey, Corey, I saw that. Don't play with me," Jackie said to him. They drove off and headed to the prom then valeted the car like they all were some type of bosses. They went to the prom, greeted their friends, and took many pictures with each other as well as with friends from school.

"Can I have this dance, sweetheart?" Jacob asked Lisa. As they danced they talked about what was going to happen after they graduated school in a few days. Lisa looked across and saw Latasha and Corey dancing and talking to each other also.

"I wonder what they are talking about to each other," she said to Jacob. "It is crazy that you and Corey will be going to different schools while Latasha and I are going to be in the same school. For the first time after all this time, we will be separated from each other."

"Well, you will be good because at least you and Latasha will still be together," Jacob replied.

"You're right about that. It would be crazy going to school without Latasha. We've been down with each other since we were nine years old and have been through a lot together."

The evening winded down and soon it was time for the announcement of the prom king and queen. Jacob and Lisa were crowned prom King and Queen and Latasha came to Lisa and said, "I knew it! Should have been me that was Queen,"she laughed.

"Well, you have to be flyer than me to win queen, Miss Thing," Lisa joked.

"Aww, you look so cute, girl. Congratulations!" Then they both hugged.

"Bro, I knew you were going to win prom King because you always be on your grown man look," Corey said to Jacob. All the ladies at school was on your top but you the holy man, which only made them want you more."

"Hey, bro, I am just sitting here thinking about how God is so good. He protected us from danger and allowed us to finish school. Do you know the judge gave Shawn 18 years for being in the car with them dudes who raped that girl? He did not even know anything about that and just for being in the car, he is doing 18 years. They tried him as an adult and now he will not be getting out until he is around 36 years old. That is crazy, bro. We are so blessed to have been covered by the blood, even when we did not do what was right in God's eyes," said Jacob.

"Yeah, bro, you are right, man, and I feel you on that," Corey said. The night finally ended and Lisa was trying to go to a hotel with Jacob. Jacob told Lisa that he was trying to continue to walk in the way of the Lord and Lisa got very upset because she was looking to end the night in an exciting way with Jacob.

Corey had been thinking about all the talks he'd been having with Pastor Mark and told Latasha that he was not going to the hotel because he was trying to get himself back on track with the Lord. As he spoke to Latasha he thought to himself that if there was anyone that really needed to start living right for the Lord it needed to be him because he still couldn't forget about the two people he murdered during the shootout alongside of Mike and his goons. Corey was thinking about what Jacob had just told him about Shawn doing 18 years in jail for a crime he did not even do and he started to think about the bodies and how much time he could have been facing if word of the murders ever got out. He believed that God may have spared him for a calling to do work for the Gospel. They all left and went home. They had the next day off to start getting ready for their graduation.

*****

A few days later, everyone was dressed up wearing their caps and gowns and ready to walk to get their diplomas. Hannah and Pastor Mark were at the school with members of the church and they were cheering the students on as they were called up for awards. They called the names of the colleges that they'd all be attending in the fall. Jacob was named class valedictorian and made an awesome speech to his senior class members. After Jacob did his speech everyone yelled and threw their caps in the air. Then Pastor Mark and Hannah got Jacob, Corey, Lisa, and Latasha together and said a prayer that they would be protected while in college and make wise decisions while away from home.

Later that day, everyone went out for dinner to celebrate. They spoke about life and how to not let the devil stop you from moving to greatness. "It's been a rough time but we're almost done, my love. Just another six more years to go," said Hannah as she looked to the sky. She believed her late husband Jacob Sr. was looking down on her and listening to her.

Chapter 8

PUTTING IN THAT WORK

Colossian 3:23 KJV

And whatsoever ye do, do it heartily, as to the Lord, and not unto men.

After two whole years had passed Jacob, Corey, Lisa, and Latasha were now sophomores in their second year of college. Everyone had been getting good grades but also had been partying very crazy as college kids normally do. Corey had been driving from his college to meet up with Jacob because his school was only an hour and 25 minutes away. His distance from Latasha was a little further since it was a little past Jacob's school. Every week they would rotate. One week Lisa and Latasha would drive to Jacob's school and Corey would meet them there, or everyone would meet Corey at his school because there were always nice parties at his school. The girls' school was too preppy to spend a lot of time there so Jacob and Corey never really liked hanging out at their school.

It was Saturday and it was Corey's birthday. Lisa's birthday was coming up in four days. Their birthdays being so close made things easy. They thought that it would be best to just all hang out and they decided to get fake IDs to get into Club Turn Up.

"Hey, where can we get fake IDs so we can get into Turn Up? I heard that club be jumping on Saturdays," Corey asked a guy named Bonnie Joe, who he heard might be able to help him.

"Well, my man, I can get you the IDs but it is going to cost you a few dollars," said Bonnie Joe.

"How much?" Corey asked.

"It'll be $100 for each one of you to get them made. They're the real deal state IDs, so when the club security scans them, they will come up legit. The security at the club be checking for fake IDs like crazy and if you get caught they will lock you right up. The club moves a lot of money and is very careful about who is coming in and out," Bonnie Joe told Corey.

"Okay, so here is $400 for all four of us. I need you to make this happen, because it is my birthday and we are all trying having a good time tonight," said Corey.

"No problem. Just bring your friends by in the next hour so I can take all you guys' pictures," Bonnie Joe said.

"Cool, I will have everyone ready and in position to move out and meet up with you in the next hour. Good looking out," Corey replied. Corey went and met up with Jacob, Lisa, and Latasha to tell them all that they owed him $100 each. He even told Latasha, his own girlfriend, that she had to pay as well. Everyone went to see Bonnie Joe to have their photos taken for their IDs. They had to write down their full names, height, and weight along with their hair and eye color.

"Alright, people, I have all the basic stuff I need from you as of now. Just come back in two hours and they will be ready," said Bonnie Joe.

"What's up? You people trying to go get some pizza and play a few video games while we all wait for the IDs?" Latasha asked everyone.

"Yeah, let's do it. I'm down with that," said Jacob.

Everyone made their way to the pizza shop, where they all ate pizza, talked, and reminisced about the old days for a little while. Finally, the group headed over to the B-side of the restaurant to play a few videos games for a little over 45 minutes. Then they headed out to meet Bonnie Joe back at his place to pick up their IDs.

"Hey, these IDs are real official. I can use this for a whole year until I really turn 21," Corey said to the group, laughing. "This means now we can get alcohol and cigarettes and get into any club we want without any issues. God is so good. Yes, He is all the time," said Corey.

"Hey, bro, do not use the Lord's name in vain because there is nothing good about what we're doing and we know that this is not right. And it really looks bad on me because look at the school I go to. Do you know where I go to school there are no clubs near campus? The closest clubs are 35 to 40 miles away?" Jacob responded back to Corey and the others.

"We understand you walk with the Lord and all that bro but right now, we trying to have a good time and either you down or you not," Corey said to Jacob.

"Whatever bro, I'm down and want to have a good time, and although I know it's nothing that I am really missing, I still would like to know what's going on and to see and have the experience."

"Say, hey young blood, you mean to tell me that you go against your own faith just to hang out at a club?" Bonnie Joe asked Jacob with a disgusted look on his face.

"No, Bonnie Joe, it is just sometimes as a young man serving the Lord and trying to live a righteous life I feel that some of my fun is taken away from me."

"Yeah, young blood, I feel you and pray that you continue to find your way."

"Hey, we out everyone and I am driving. Thanks, Bonnie Joe for looking out with these IDs and I will be putting my friends onto you for more," said Lisa.

"Remember, if any of you are caught with these IDs you did not get them from me or my people. It's on you," said Bonnie Joe.

"A'ight, my man, we got you but in the meantime, we out. We got to get dressed so we can roll out. I will holla at you some time next week so you can make IDs for my other friends. Peace," said Corey. Everyone drove in Lisa's car and headed over to Corey's apartment to take showers and get dressed to be fresh for Club Turn Up.

"Hey, Dad, what's up? How are you and when can I come to Miami to hang out with you?" Jacob was in the other room in Corey's apartment listening to Latasha on the phone with her dad and he could hear him screaming at the top of his lungs about some money he heard Corey had that belonged to him. As Latasha was trying to play it off by asking Mike what he was talking about Jacob walked in and Latasha rushed her dad off the phone, telling him that she would call him later and that she loved him and to be safe.

"You mean to tell me Mike's been asking you about the money that he is missing the whole time?" Jacob asked Latasha with an angry look. She has kept this big secret from everyone for the past two years.

"Yes, Jacob, and I am sorry I kept this from the rest of you but I didn't want anyone to worry because things have been so quiet since Big Rome and my dad have been on the run. I just want to continue to keep the drama at zero as long as I can. We only have two more years left in school and you still have four years left but when Corey and I finish school we should be able to pay back the money. It is not as if Corey just took the $65,000 and did not use it for good."

"You know what, Latasha? You are right but just think about what your dad would do to someone that took

109

$65,000 of his money while he's back in Miami doing whatever he can to survive while on a run for a few murders?"

Latasha started to look very puzzled and walked away as she started to think.

"Hey, whoever is next to use the shower go ahead and use it now because the water is starting to get a little cold. We need to get there on time because the line for the club is going to be very long. Everyone is going to be there since it's the first opening of the summer," said Lisa.

"Yeah, I am getting in the shower next," said Latasha. As she was walking into the bathroom Corey noticed a puzzled look on her face and asked her what was going on. Latasha told Corey everything was okay and then she closed the bathroom door to get in the shower. As Latasha was taking her shower she was just thinking about how her dad's tone was while she was talking to him on the phone.

Finally, everyone was dressed and they headed out to go to Club Turn Up. As they arrived at the club, they could see that the line to get in was very long. The line was so long that it wrapped around the corner.

"I can't take this. I am cutting the line. I need to be in here like ASAP because if we wait in this line by the time we get in the place will be closed," said Corey.

"What do you suggest we do? There is no other way but to wait like everyone else is doing," said Jacob.

"Oh but there is a way and I think I know just where Corey is going with this," said Lisa. "We are going to pay the bouncer to cut the line because money talks."

"Well, okay, how about Corey and I try this first and then the two of you come if you see us get in?" said Latasha.

"That sounds like a great plan so you two go ahead and we will be right behind you," Jacob replied. Corey and Latasha walked to the front and then Latasha whispered in one of the bouncer's ears as Corey shook the other bouncer's hand very smoothly to slide money in his palm. It was one hundred dollars for him and Latasha. The bouncer lifted up the rope and let them both in to the club.

"Wow, that's crazy. Come on, Lisa, so we can get in. You look stunning so take the money and do the same thing," said Jacob as he passed his woman one hundred dollars. Lisa repeated the same process as Latasha, only she was the one putting the money in the bouncer's hand. Then her and Jacob walked right in after the bouncer lifted up the rope for them.

Finally, everyone was in Club Turn up dancing, drinking, and having a good time. "Hey, bartender, let me get two shots of vodka with a hit of Cherry Coke on the rocks," requested Lisa.

" Basically, you just want two rum and Cokes," said the bartender.

"Yeah, I guess," Lisa replied to the bartender, smiling to hide her clueless look. She did not want the bartender to know that it was her first time there or find out that she was really underage. Lisa got the drinks, drank them both, and then asked Jacob what he was drinking.

"I will have just a Cherry Coke to drink, sir," said Jacob to the bartender.

Everyone was buying drinks and really turning up except Jacob because he was already feeling convicted in his heart about being in the club. He knew it was not Christ-like at all. Hannah's voice kept coming in his head about following her as she follows Christ and if she ever stopped following Christ to turn the other way. She'd told him if he saw something that was not lined up with the Word of God or not Christ-like to turn the other way. Those were some of the basics that his mother told him to really try to remember.

As the night went on at the club and everyone was having a good time, suddenly, a fight broke out and then out of nowhere loud gunshots could be heard going off. Jacob could see a person trying to grab Corey, so Jacob punched him in the face, and then two other people came out of nowhere and grabbed Jacob. One of the people was holding Jacob and the other people were punching him. Then Lisa reached for a beer bottle that was sitting on the bar and cracked one of the guys in the head with it, shattering glass everywhere. She was grabbed into the crowd and started fighting with a woman that was dressed like a man. Latasha was lost in the crowd looking for everyone as the whole club was going wild and totally chaotic. A man grabbed her but she managed to break free and run back the other way that she came from only to see Lisa fighting the woman dressed like a dude. Latasha and Lisa were now fighting the woman together.

Meanwhile, the bouncers were making their way in and the fighting stopped as they swept the club, looking for anyone that was involved in the shootout and brawl. Corey made his way to Lisa and Latasha and the three of them left through the back doorway.

"Hey, where is Jacob? I did not see him leave the club and the police are on their way here. We need to find him right away because none of us are legal," said Lisa. Lisa went back into the club and found Jacob laying on the ground, knocked unconscious under a table. Lisa crawled her way to the back door and yelled for Corey to tell him that she found Jacob but she needed help getting him out. Corey and Latasha came back into the club with Lisa and the three of them dragged Jacob out of the club. They tried to get him to wake up but he was not responding. Finally, after several minutes, Jacob started to stand. Lisa shook him gently and called his name to fully wake him up. Jacob looked up and saw everyone.

"What the heck is going on? Where am I?" Jacob asked as he starts to stand to his feet. The last thing I can remember is fighting two people because another person was trying to grab you Corey," said Jacob.

"Yeah, man, it was a big fight that jumped off in the club. I guess one of them thought that I was involved and tried to grab me, and that is where you came in," said Corey.

"I just got the word that two people died from gunshot wounds. It is time for us to go and get out of here," said Lisa. Jacob, Lisa, Latasha, and Corey get to their car and Jacob drives, as he is the only one who did not drink any alcohol. They drove back to Corey's apartment and ordered pizza to eat so that no one went to bed on an empty stomach.

"Yeah, I hate to bust you peoples' fun but tomorrow I have to start studying for my finals that are coming up in the next two weeks," said Jacob.

"Yeah, I feel you on that Jacob. I will be doing the same thing tomorrow," said Latasha.

"You people are starting to be too played out talking about going back to your dorms to study," said Corey.

"Do you know once again today we were all blessed because one of us could have lost our life? It seems like every time one of us starts to do something that does not line up with God and we experience a life or death situation, God gets us out of it. There is a purpose for each and every one of us and that is all I am going to say. I am not going to sit here and try to preach because I will be sitting here all day, but we need to count our blessings," said Jacob.

When they woke up the next morning, everyone packed up, said goodbye to Corey with hugs, and headed back to school to start studying for their finals. Corey started to feel down because he would be alone again. Jacob was alright being alone at his own school because some of the students were becoming close friends with him as he built new relationships with new brothers and sisters at his Bible school. Lisa and Latasha were becoming closer than ever because they were in the same school and to make it better their dorm rooms were in the same building right down the hall from each other's.

Jacob was getting more into the Word and learning how to build a better relationship with Jesus as his prayer advanced more and more. Jacob started off with 20 minutes of prayer but now he was able to talk to the Lord more because he had been putting in work with praying more. Jacob knew that there was a lot more work for him to do if he wanted to be preaching the Gospel like his father did, and he knew that he needed to yell to the Lord more to continue to fight the temptation of the devil.

When Jacob got back to campus, he decided to give Pastor Mark a phone call for spiritual guidance.

"Hey, brother, how are you doing in school and what's new in your life? How is your walk with the Lord and how are your grades?" Pastor Mark asked Jacob and Jacob told him everything was okay. "Let us say a quick prayer before we talk," said Pastor Mark. They prayed and then started to talk. "Hey, Jacob, your mother told me not to tell you because she did not want you to be worried, but brace yourself for what I am about to tell you."

"What is it, Pastor Mark? Please tell me because I really need to know," said Jacob.

"Your mother has stomach cancer and has been in and out of the hospital for the last two months." Jacob started to break down in tears. His mother was his best friend and biggest supporter. He had a great relationship with Hannah.

"I don't understand. Why hasn't she called me to tell me? Maybe I can leave school and take care of her until she gets better. How will I focus now when I will be thinking about her health?" said Jacob.

"This is the reason why your mother could not tell you. Because she knows you would start getting worried and lose focus in school. Just remember we serve an awesome God and he is a healer! Open your Bible, Jacob." Pastor Mark gave him a powerful scripture to stick with him; one to lift his spirit up and stop him from worrying. Jacob hung up the phone and then he started to pray and ask the Lord for answers.

"Dear God, why? How can you let this happen after my mother has been serving you all these years? My mom's been a good servant to you and your Word and put in a lot of work while walking in your Word. All I have is my mother and now you're trying to take her away from me. You already allowed my father to die and I could not be too upset with that because I never knew my father. My mother has been taking care of me as a single parent for years and never complained, even when she worked and slaved herself like a dog just to keep food on the table.

116

This is not fair, God. I work so hard to live a righteous life and this is what you give me in return? My mother with stomach cancer? As Jacob prayed, crying to the Lord, he fell asleep and fell into a deep dream. In the dream he saw him and his father and mother having a family dinner and fellowshipping together like they were having some kind of family devotion. The dream seemed so real to Jacob because it was the closest that he had ever been to his father.

Jacob's alarm went off to let him know that it was time for him to start studying for his finals. He really wanted to call his mother but decided to wait until the time was right to call her and ask her why she did not tell him that she was sick. Jacob started to get focused and study for his finals. He really needed to study to pass because his family and church family had already invested a lot of money for him to finish school.

Jacob studied and studied and felt he was ready to take the finals that same day but nevertheless he still continued to study to make sure he knew everything that would be on the finals in all his classes for sure. Finally, Jacob put his books to the side and called his mother up.

"Hey, son, how are you doing? Is everything okay," Hannah asked.

"No, mom. What is this that I hear that you got stomach cancer?" Why haven't you told me instead of waiting until I heard it from Pastor Mark? It would had been better if I had heard it from you," said Jacob.

"Son, you are right. I should have told you already but I wanted Pastor Mark to tell you first because I knew that you would really listen to him and I did not want you to lose focus on what you got going on in your life. What you have to understand, son, is that you are becoming a young mighty man of God and I may really be gone from this earth soon. We both know God is a healer but if it is not in His will for me to live, He will call me home to be in glory with your father. The only way you will be able to see us is to continue to walk in the light and finish the works of the Lord. You must stay with Jesus until the end when He calls you home. I may not be here on this earth for much longer but I will be in glory where I will not have to worry about paying bills or getting sick anymore. I will not have anymore suffering in my body and no more pain," said Hannah.

"Yeah, but what am I going to do when you're gone? How will I continue to live life without you, Mom? It is going to be hard to move on, knowing that you will not be here," said Jacob.

"My baby boy, you will be fine. You are growing up to be a mighty man of God and will have to lean on the Lord for you answers. Continue to seek His Word and pray for all understanding in your life. If there is anything I want you to remember from me it is to pray before making any decision in your life. You must trust in the Lord at all times, even in bad times. God does not make mistakes. He knows what He is doing so trust in Him, my son."

"So what have the doctors been saying about your cancer? Have they found a way to treat it? Are you getting better?"

"Well, the doctors are telling me that I only have eight months to live and I will be gone from this earth then. I do not listen to the doctors' reports because I believe in the report from the Lord. We have to learn not to listen and trust in man because they will fail you all the time. We have to learn to listen and trust in the Lord at all times."

"Hey, Mom, how is it that your faith is so strong and you never worry about things?" Jacob asked his mother with tears in his eyes on the other end of the phone line.

"I will tell you a quick story, son, and this is a story I really want you to remember. Your father and I were living in our first apartment together and a year after we got married your father lost his job. We had only one month's rent saved up and the rent was due in like eight days. We had no other income but the money we would pay for tithes. Your dad said that he believed in God and knew He would provide for us. He then told me that he was going to put all of our money that we had saved up for rent and bills into tithes. I looked at him and asked him if he was crazy and he told me that he was very crazy for the Lord. He told me that he would just trust in the Lord and told me he wanted to show me how God moves when you listen to him. He told me that the Holy Spirit told him to put all the money into the tithe basket on the upcoming Sunday and then fast and pray for one week. Your father was very obedient and listened to the Word from the Lord and did just what he was told. The next week in Sunday service,

119

there was a man who joined the church. He was tired of all the sinning that he was doing and wanted to turn his life around for good. The second Sunday he came to our church he asked if we could pray that his son would be led to Jesus along with him. His wife was just murdered because of the things that he was doing in the streets. Your father was asked by our pastor to pray for the man and his son. The man was in his late 30s and his son was around 17 years old but was in the streets with his dad moving crazy drugs and owned almost half the town. The third Sunday the man and his son showed up to church and the man had so much joy on his face. It was as if a weight was lifted off of him because he seemed so peaceful. In fact, he was so happy he started to talk to your father after church and then pulled out a white envelope. He said the Lord had told him to bless your father with that and that he was just listening to what God told him to do. Inside the envelope, there was a certified check for $42,000. Your dad was so shocked because it was part of his prayer to the Lord that he could be able to start his own church. He needed the financial blessing. Our loving pastor Jon was ready to step down because the Lord was telling him to hand the church over to a new upcoming mighty man of God and that was your father. Pastor Jon wanted to spend more time with his family, as they were not getting to see him most of the time due to the work he was doing for the church. Your father fasted, prayed, and got a financial blessing because he listened to the Holy Spirit and did what the Lord told him to do. The person that gave your father the check was Mark Sr., the father of Pastor Mark."

"Wow, so you mean to tell me Pastor Mark has been in the picture with our family this long?"

"Yes, son, and as time passed, about 12 years before you were born, Mark Sr. went home to be with the Lord. He died of brain cancer. Right before he went home to be with the Lord he asked your father to watch out for his son and show him the way of Jesus Christ and equip him with the Word of God so he can be a mighty man of God. That is what your father did-raised Pastor Mark like his little brother into the Gospel so that he could train other people. Your father became the pastor and had over 1,200 members. Finally, I was pregnant with you and your father was rushing to see me deliver you and was killed in a tragic car accident right outside the hospital you were born in. While I was delivering you, he was dead in the room down the hall from us. Pastor Mark rushed to the hospital and then told me the news after you were delivered. A week and two days later, we had a big home going for your dad and it was like a big parade. About a month later, bills were crazy and we needed to keep the church going and pay for all your father's expenses so instead of Pastor Mark trusting the Lord, he hooked up with a childhood friend and that was Mike. Pastor Mark was back in the streets heavy but knew that he was doing by God and your father because he told your father that he would look out for you and show you the way of the Lord way before your father passed away. After working in the streets with Mike, Pastor Mark was able to help me pay off the bills. Later he got into shootouts, took lives, and him and Mike even left Big Rome for dead. Finally, the feds ran down on Pastor Mark and Mike, and they were both locked up. Rather than becoming a rat and telling on Mike, Pastor Mark did a few years in prison, where he rededicated his life to Jesus Christ and started to walk a stronger walk with him. The time moved on and Pastor Mark was ready to become the pastor for our church. You see, you never know what God has in store for you so this is the reason why we must allow the Holy Spirit to lead and guide us to true understanding."

"Wow, so you mean to tell me that our church where Pastor Mark preaches was my father's church first?"

"That's right. Pastor Mark's father gave your father the financial blessing and then when Mark Sr. passed away to be home with the Lord, your father helped raise up Pastor Mark and then left the church to him in his will so that if he ever passed away to be with the Lord then Pastor Mark would take over the church. The only catch to your father signing the will over to Pastor Mark was that he help raise you up as a mighty man of God and then leave the church to you when you are ready."

"This is one of the greatest stories that I've ever heard and it is a true story. Wow, I really needed to hear this, Mom. I am starting to feel a lot better but I have a few confessions to make to you first before I get back into studying for my finals."

"Okay, but let me ask you, did you already confess with God? Did you ask for his forgiveness before confessing to me?"

"Yes, I did, Mom."

"So what is the confession that you want to make with me, Jacob?" Hannah asked.

"I've been having a lot of sex with Lisa and I got a fake ID and went into a club and got in a crazy fight. Me, Corey, Lisa, and Latasha were there and we all were fighting. I was knocked out unconscious for a while. There were gunshots fired with people running for their lives and all. A couple of people were killed right on the scene."

"Do you see how God works, Jacob? That could have been you and you could have ended your life in the wrong place. That would have been hell if you would have died in your sin without a chance for repentance. Whether i I'm here with you or not you really have to listen to the voice of God and do the right thing, Jacob, and that is living a Godly life unto him. The devil came to steal, kill, and destroy but God came to give you life to live more abundantly. You do not have any business being in a club or having sex with Lisa without being married to her, Jacob. What if you got her pregnant? You have to finish school because people are counting on you, including your father. It was some of his money that was invested in your education as well."

"Hey, Mom, I hear you but it is not like I be having sex with Lisa unprotected. The reason why I do is that Lisa keeps telling me that she will find a new boyfriend if I do not."

"Well if Lisa is talking like that then she does not really love you or care about your walk with the Lord. If

FREDERICK B. RUSH JR.

you really love Lisa then you should put a ring on it and ask to marry her. First out of respect, you have to ask her parents if you can marry her. Once you get their approval then you need to ask Lisa. God really honors marriage and it is okay to have all the sex you want if you two are married."

"I wanted to ask her to marry me but I wanted her to be almost finished school because I wanted her to focus on her education first. I know how women can get. Once I propose then I have to worry about her looking around for a wedding dress and making plans for the wedding and it will take her mind off school so I wanted to wait a little longer."

"If you plan to wait a little longer then you better not be having anymore sex with her until you get married to her. If you continue to sleep with her before getting married to her then your marriage could be cursed and not blessed. I know people say that it is not true and just an old saying but it is real. You have to stand your ground, son, and be encouraged unto the things of God, as sin is only for a season."

"Okay, Mom, I will continue to pray and do right by the Lord and keep working hard to make you proud. Whatever you do just do not die on me. I want you to see me get married and have kids and become the preacher you and dad want me to become. I love you, Mom. Get some rest and feel better, and if you need me for anything just call me and I will be there."

"Thanks, son. I love you too and will continue to pray for you that God will watch over you and keep you safe. You better stay out them clubs boy or I am going to come to your school and whip you with my new belt," said Hannah, laughing. Hannah and Jacob closed their conversation with a nice prayer and then Jacob continued to study for his finals.

*****

A few days later Jacob took his finals and passed with straight As. He was so happy to call the rest of the gang to see what they'd gotten on their finals. Lisa got a few As and a few Bs. Corey had gotten all Bs on his finals and Latasha got an A, two Bs, and a C. Jacob's grade point average was still at 4.0 and he continued to thank the Lord for allowing it to happen by giving Him all the glory. The school was finally closing down for the summer and all the college students were headed home for the summer break. Jacob spoke to the gang and planned to meet at Lisa's to plan a surprise birthday party for his mother.

Jacob and the rest of his friends met at Lisa's house to talk about having the surprise 60th birthday party for his mother. Hannah did not have a clue that she would be having a birthday party. Jacob called friends and people from the church to invite them to the birthday party. Lisa called the DJ and the florist to decorate the tables. Latasha was calling to book the location that would hold 200 or more guests. She was calling different places to get the best price that she could get. Finally, Corey called to get the catered food and birthday cake delivered to the location that Latasha had picked.

"My son, if you need help paying for this just let me know and I will help," said Lisa's father.

"Thanks, sir, I may hold you to that because I might need a little help from you," Jacob said.

*****

Finally, a week had gone by and the day was finally here. It was Hannah's 60th birthday.

"Hey, Mom, come on. We are going to be late for our dinner reservation," said Jacob.

"Come on, son, you keep rushing me as if I am one of the Rushes. I will be down in a few minutes." Several minutes later, Hannah came down the steps wearing a nice gold dress with the gold pumps and handbag to match. Her makeup was well done and she looked like she was in her early 30s. You could not tell that she was turning 60. As she stepped out of Jacob's car in front of the building you could hear men whistling and acting crazy, lusting over her as if she was a piece of meat.

"Hey, ma, you bad. Can I get your number? We can come back here on our next date," one young man said.

Hannah looked at the young man and told him he better be worrying about going on a date with Jesus. As Hannah walked into the building with Jacob, a photographer took pictures of her and Jacob. Then she looked up and saw someone holding a video camera

"Jacob, what is this you got me into, boy?" she asked.

"SURPRISE!"

Hannah was stunned to see everyone she knew there. She was never expecting it. She was only expecting to share her birthday with her only son. "Wow, son, you got me this time and later you have to tell me how you did it."

"Well, Mom, I will be more than happy to tell you later on, but in the meantime just enjoy your birthday because you can only turn 60 once in your life. Happy birthday, Mom, and I love you," said Jacob as he grabbed his mother and gave her a big hug and kiss. Everyone started to dance and then Pastor Mark showed up and gave a great speech about Hannah and how long they'd known each other.

Hannah spoke to everyone and thanked them sincerely and she then gave her testimony about the battle she was having with stomach cancer. "The cancer is not that aggressive yet, the doctors have said. I want to pray it out of my body before it gets aggressive. I was scared a little when I first heard about it and was not too happy but then I started thinking about God's Word and how much of a healer he is. I just started to worship him right in the doctor's office. They were looking at me as if I was crazy as I stood up and said, *today is the day for salvation. Do not look at me as if I am crazy I have all my marbles. I just feel sorry for the people who do not know the Lord Jesus as their God*," said Hannah. "Now let's finish partying!"

127

Finally, as the night was ending the host brought out a huge cake with a big "60" on the top. It was vanilla buttercream and chocolate flavored. The cake had whipped cream designed in the shape of angels on it. The lights were turned off and they came by to light the candles on the cake. Then everyone sang Happy Birthday to Hannah. Pastor Mark pulled out a flash drive and plugged it into the computer that was hooked up to the projector. When he pressed play, it was a video message from the late Jacob Sr.

"Hey, babe, I know when you see this tears may come quick to you. Hello, son, this is your daddy. Yes, it is really me if you're asking yourself that but right now I just wanted to take the time to wish my beautiful wife a happy 60th birthday. May the Lord continue to keep you. I know I am not physically there with you two but I am there in spirit right now. I want to share a quick testimony for everyone who is watching this right now. When the Holy Spirit speaks so clearly to you and tells you to do something then you really should do it. I recorded this video because I was led to do this and if you're watching this video you can see how God moves. I never knew that I would be home with the Lord so early but God does not make any mistakes. If I was alive and on earth you would not have seen this video. Be encouraged and follow God. I followed him until I was called to glory. Son, I am counting on you to make the right decisions and do what is right. If what you're doing does not line up with God and His Word, you have to turn the other way because it can be a trick of the devil. Hannah, I love you. Keep pressing in Jesus and I will see you when you get to heaven. I will be waiting to see you in glory with our Lord and Savior Jesus

Christ. Happy 60th birthday and make sure you get some rest."

The video was dated September 1, 1979, four days before Jacob Jr. was born. Hannah was crying tears of joy. "Oh my God, he recorded this four days before he died," Hannah stated in shock.

"Yes, Hannah," said Pastor Mark, "and he only wanted me to show you this when you turned 60 years old."

"Wow, I finally was able to really see and hear my dad talk to me for the first time ever," said Jacob, as he also cried tears of joy.

As the cake was cut and passed around to everyone, Corey came over to tell Jacob that he heard Big Rome was running the streets again. He had come back from his sister's house and was looking for him, Mike, and the other members from the crew to finally finish the beef.

"Corey, after experiencing what I've just experienced I am not worrying about Big Rome. We can talk about that tomorrow or later. In the meanwhile, let this day stay a good day without any negativity," said Jacob.

"Yeah, you're right bro, but we're going to finish this conversation later because I may need to get my hands on a few new pistols," said Corey.

After everyone left the party, Jacob took Hannah home and noticed there was a black SUV sitting across the street from his house. "Mom, go into the house. I want to take a look at that black SUV," said Jacob.

"Hey, do not do anything stupid, Jacob," said Hannah. As Jacob walked to the black SUV the window rolled down and it was Mike.

"What is up, little homie? We need to have a real talk. Get in the car," said Mike.

"No, I am not going to get in your car," said Jacob.

"I'm not asking you, I'm telling you to get in the car now," said Mike. Jacob got into the car and then Mike had him call Hannah to tell her that it was one of his friends from college and that he would be in the house soon.

"Mike, what do you want from me, man? Why am I here?"

"What do you think?" Mike laughed. "Where is my $65,000? And where is Big Rome?"

"I don't know where Big Rome is but Corey told me earlier that the word on the streets is that he is out and looking for you."

"Give this to Corey and tell him to call me," Mike said, handing Jacob a small bag and a business card with a new number on it. He then showed Jacob an ID with Mike's photo but Pastor Mark's name. Mike started to laugh hard. "I am with the Lord now, just like you, li'l homie." Jacob gave Mike a disgusted look.

"Can I go now, man?" Jacob asked.

"Yeah, go on, but don't forget to give Corey my message. We got a lot of catching up to do and many things to talk about."

Chapter 9

STREET FAME

Matthew 4:4 KJV

But he answered and said, It is written, Man shall not live by bread alone, but by every word that proceeded out of the mouth of God.

The next morning came and Jacob was awakened by a loud bang on the door. It was Corey asking to come in because he wanted to talk. Corey was breathing fast and sweating. He said that he needed to strap up with some burners because he had seen Big Rome and his goons and they started shooting at him while he was coming from the store for his mother. He saw Big Rome but thought Big Rome didn't see him. Then the next thing he knew he heard shots. One bullet just missed him by a few inches. It was very close to hitting him in the shoulder. "From there I just came straight over here to your house," said Corey to Jacob.

"Hey, you do not need guns to protect you because Jesus is your protection," said Jacob.

"Look, bro, where was Jesus like 25 minutes ago when I was running for my life? I just saw my whole life flash before my eyes and I did not see Jesus at all. I am starting to get a little tired of you talking all holy, bro, because at the end of the day you're my man and if Big Rome can't get to me then he will be trying to get at you and I can't have that. It is time we finally end Big Rome. You're either going to ride with me or not because the time has come and we're about to be at war, picking up from where we left off last time. This is part two but this time we cannot take any losses. This dude killed my little sister years ago, shot at me, and killed some good brothers that I was cool with. We have to do this whether you like it or not. I hear what you saying about Jesus being my protection, but I am just saying where was He when Big Rome had the drop on me and was ready to take me out?" Corey said, speaking with much frustration.

"Hey, look, bro, you talking about you hear me but you don't really hear me. It is all a trap and a trick of the devil to get you all worked up so you'll do something stupid. You have to be wiser and see the setup before you act. Then again, you never think anyway. All you do is operate off of your emotions and make wrong decisions. Come on, Corey, you've been like this all your life. On top of that, God bailed you out with those bodies you dropped; you are blessed that you're not doing life right now. Look at all the good God is doing for us now. We all are about to finish college in a few more years and make something out of ourselves. Only the strong and smart people will survive, bro. That is why you have to allow yourself to stay connected to God and not allow the devil to trick or trap you up. By the way, Mike was waiting outside my house last night and he knows about the $65,000 you took from him, and he wants it back. He said for you to call him using the burner phone that he gave you a while ago and he gave me this to give to you," Jacob said, handing Corey the business card and small bag. Inside of the bag was a chrome 40 caliber gun with two extra full clips and $500 cash wrapped in a rubber band. On the business card was a phone number and the location of the hotel where Mike was currently staying.

"Hey, bro, I am out," said Corey. "I will have to go and let Mike know that I used his money for school. I am ready to handle the consequences that come," said Corey.

"No, bro, wait. I can't let you go see Mike alone. I would not be a real friend if I did that. I am going with you. At least it will be two against one," said Jacob.

When Corey and Jacob finally got Mike on the phone he told them to meet him at his laundromat located on 31st Street. When they arrived at the laundromat, they were greeted by an old man who directed them to the back of the laundromat. As they sat down Mike lifted his head and looked Corey dead in his eyes.

"Where is my money?" he asked Corey.

"Mike, I have to be real with you, man. When the feds raided the shop they didn't really do a good job searching the place. I went back a few days later to see what they'd found and was just looking around. As I was looking around, I went into the basement and found your money that you had stashed away. My intentions were not to keep your money; it was just to hold your money," said Corey.

FREDERICK B. RUSH JR.

"So, what did you do with my money, li'l homie? Because right about now I really need it. It's about to be on again with this dude Big Rome and we have to finish this once and for all," said Mike.

"Well, I had to use the money for school. I just wanted to do right by myself and I did not know how to get in contact with you because you were on the run from the law. I promise if you spare me I will get the money back to you as soon as I can," said Corey.

"Look, li'l homie, I am not going to do anything to you because you're almost my son-in-law. As long as you keep my little girl happy you are family," said Mike.

"Thank you. I really appreciate it coming from you, sir. I have about $22,000 that I flipped for you while I was away at school," said Corey.

"Well, I am very impressed with you, Corey, and I knew you would not leave me empty-handed. I knew that you would come up with some way to make it right. Give me the money because I really need it right now. I need all the money I can get to flip because it's about to be on this time," said Mike.

"Hey, why do you need to do that, Mike? Why can't you just stay in the cut like you were doing in Miami? You used a new ID with a new name and things have been very quiet these past few years," Jacob said.

"Look, preacher boy, I am not trying to hear anything about God or peace right now because Big Rome killed many of my people and now it is time for him to

136

meet Satan face to face to pay for the sins that he committed," Mike said.

"Wow, look who is talking about paying for their sins. What you think you've been doing the whole time, Mike, and why do you think you are in this situation? You are just as wrong as Big Rome is, and two wrongs do not make a right. You killed some of his people too and left him for dead. Did you think he was going to let you get away with that?" said Jacob.

"What are you, one of Big Rome's groupies or something? Why are you defending him, li'l homie? That dude needs to go. It is just his time."

"Look, I am not defending him. It's just that this is going to a whole new level between the two of you and someone innocent might catch a bullet for something that has nothing to do with them at all, just like Corey's little sister. It time to stop worrying about earning street fame and think about the lives that you may be taking when you pull that trigger, Mike. One day there will be a time when you will have to stand before God and He will want answers about why you took part in such acts. There will be no justifying the choices that you made, so if I were you I would rethink what I am about to do before moving out."

"Okay, I hear you, young blood, but as I think, I only see death for Big Rome. I see nothing but trying to get him out of here for good."

"You're right, man. When it is time for you to get out of here you just have to get out of here," said Corey, laughing as he gives Mike a high-five.

"See, that's why I really like you, Corey. You got a lot of heart and do not really care. You make moves by living life by the day and your man needs to learn from you. He would be a lot better off," said Mike to Corey.

"No, I am better off with Jesus and that is where I choose to stay. If people do not like me for what I am, I will let it be known that I stand for Jesus and I do not try to impress anyone else. As long as I stand for Jesus and impress him then I am good to go."

"Well, we're about to stand for ourselves and get back into the mix with these dudes because we have to put this to rest today," said Mike.

"I will keep you in my prayers, Mike, and pray that you find it in your heart to change for the Lord," Jacob said.

"Okay, you two can go now and Corey, just make sure that you check back with me later on so that we can make moves," said Mike.

As Jacob and Corey left the laundromat, Jacob told Corey how he should not get involved with what is about to go down between Mike and Big Rome because God had already bailed him out before by showing him mercy. The Lord had saved him from going to prison and serving time.

Corey replied that this had to end so he could move on because he would not be walking down the street every day having to always look over his shoulder to see if someone was trying to sneak attack him.

"Well, Corey, you do what you want to do because all I know is that I will not be caught up in this mess. I have my whole life to think about and I have a lot to lose, so if you want to work for Mike again you go right ahead."

As Jacob and Corey were on their way back to Jacob's house they saw a police car and an ambulance outside of his house. Jacob ran down the street to his house and saw his mother being carried out of the house on a stretcher and put into the back of the ambulance.

"Is she okay? What happened?!" he asked Pastor Mark, who was standing outside the house.

"Hey, Jacob, I got here as fast as I could. Your mother and I were on the phone talking and of a sudden, she started to have trouble breathing. I put her on hold and then called 911 for someone to get to her house and help. Then I clicked over and told your mother I was on my way over that's why I am here now," Pastor Mark replied.

"Let's ride together and follow the ambulance to the hospital," said Jacob to Pastor Mark.

"Hold on, people. I am coming with you because Ms. Hannah is like a mother to me too," said Corey.

"Look, bro, I am not trying to be smart and don't take this any type of way but I can not have you come with me right now. You have killing and death in your heart right now and I can not have that type of energy around my mother. I don't want those type of vibes around her. My mother would love for you to see her but I never told her what type of stuff that you are into or what you have going on with Mike since he came back into the picture," said Jacob.

"What do you mean? Is this true, Corey? When we talked last we spoke about becoming mighty men of God and setting examples for others. We spoke about making the right decisions when choosing our own paths," said Pastor Mark. "I do not know how many times we have to keep going over this stuff, young man. I already told you that the devil is only out to steal, kill, and destroy but God gives you the life to live. Jacob, I think we need to let Corey ride with us because we really need to talk some Godly sense into him."

As they were in the car on the way to the hospital Pastor Mark was talking to Jacob and Corey about making the right decisions and how they should always walk into the work of the Lord. He spoke about how they needed to continue to trust and believe in God because there was a lot of sin changing the world. "These days it's hard to walk outside of your house without getting involved in some type of street drama," Pastor Mark said. "Can't you young brothers see that we are in our last days and Jesus is ready to come back sooner than you really know it? All this stuff is in the Word of God and has started happening as spoken by the Lord."

As everyone finally got to the hospital, they had to wait in the waiting room until the doctor was ready to talk to them. Pastor Mark asked everyone to say a strong prayer for Hannah as the doctor was seeing her. Lisa and Latasha finally showed up to the hospital along with Lisa's parents and everyone continued to pray.

After hours went by the doctor finally came out with the news. He told them that Hannah was fine but she would need to spend a few days in the hospital to start her chemotherapy treatment.

"Hey, doc, will this chemotherapy help my mom get better?"

"Yes, this will help treat her cancer to make her stronger, but in the meantime, make sure that you try to spend as much time with her as you can because your mother's health is starting to fail and by the looks of her, she could go any day," the doctor said to Jacob.

"Well, we're not going to listen to that report because we believe in the report from the Lord," Jacob replied.

"It is a lot to deal with right now, Jacob. Believe me, I know. We just have to continue to pray for God's mercy to allow your mother to live longer because there are still a few more things that have to be done before that happens. So just pray and believe, young man. You will be okay. We are all here for you and all praying for you," said Pastor Mark.

"You can go in and see Hannah now but only two at a time," the doctor said.

Finally, everyone went and visited Hannah in pairs of two. Jacob wanted to be the last person because he wanted to have a conversation with his mother.

141

"Hey, son, how are you doing today? I really hope you are not getting upset because as I told you before, this is all God's will and when it's my time, it is my time. I am feeling very tired and I am really trying my best to hold on for you, son. All I want is to see you finish school, get married, and start preaching the Gospel. The best thing you can do for me is to keep praying to the Lord that He will give me the extra strength to hold on, at least until you do those things," Hannah said.

"I know, Mom, and I will continue to keep praying, but on the other end, I am scared because I do not know what I will do without you. It will be very hard living a young life without you around. I am too young to lose my mom and not have you witness my success from God," said Jacob.

"Listen, son, God makes no mistakes and everything happens for a reason. If you want me to stay around this is on you and all about your prayer life with the Lord. I believe this is a test for you from God to see how much your prayer life can change. It's time, son. It is time for you to pray like you've never prayed before if you want me to be around. Trust and believe in Him and you will see the results when I am not laying up in a hospital bed."

"We can start by you praying with me right now." Jacob grabbed Hannah's hand and started to pray a very powerful prayer. After he prayed he told his mother to get some rest and gave her a kiss on her cheek. He told her he would come back and check on her within the next 12 hours.

As Jacob was leaving his mother's hospital room, Corey's phone rang and it was Mike telling him that they had to meet up. Lisa and Latasha went home with Lisa's parents and Jacob left with Pastor Mark. As they were walking out they saw Mike pull up to the hospital to pick Corey up.

"So, young brother, none of the stuff I was telling you has sunk into your head?" Pastor Mark asked.

"Look, Pastor Mark, I am not your brother and I want revenge for my little sister. You are part of the reason why my sister is dead so how dare you to try to speak to me to tell me to chill? If you and Jacob are smart then you both will strap up because if Big Rome sees either of you he is going to try to kill you," said Corey.

"Young brother, you do not even have a clue. I fight with the Word as my weapon, not a gun; and you should be doing the same."

Mike jumped out the car and started yelling at Pastor Mark. "Go ahead with all that preacher talk, Mark. No one wants to hear that crap. You're soft now, man. The Mark I used to know would let his gun clap and did not take anything from anyone. You're a sell-out that has me out here going to war while you're living for the Lord as you ride around thinking life is sweet. You are going to have drama coming your way soon, whether it is from Big Rome or me, but you better hope Big Rome gets to you first."

"Mike, are you threatening me? Because I can end you tonight."

"What if I am? What are you going to do? Call the police on me?"

"Mike, I can touch you in many ways that you can't imagine but I choose not to because I leave it up to God. You are not worth blowing my testimony, so I's rather leave you in the hands of the Lord. I will continue to keep praying for you and I still love you. I never stopped, even if you do not feel the same about me. I just want to speak nothing but blessings in your life."

"Yeah, man, you do that. We will deal with this later. We have somewhere to be so peace."

Mike drove off with Corey and Pastor Mark drove off with Jacob. As Mike and Corey were riding they spotted Big Rome and his goons' new hangout spot and now Mike had the drop on them. Mike drove to Light-skinned Chris' house to get a few pistols and a couple of brand new AKs. As Mike and Corey left Light-skinned Chris' house, Mike called the team to get together for a meeting in his office in the back of the laundromat.

"Hey, listen up, everyone. Today, we end this because we have to. As many of you know, I was on the run for a few years because of our last bang out. We have to do this but do this neatly, not sloppily. We're going to go and spray on these busters and kill everyone. I do not care who is in the way. If anyone is in the way that just means they are at the wrong place at the wrong time. A bullet has no name on it so if they know they don't belong there then they better not be there because we're spitting at everything that's in the way," said Mike, speaking to all his goons as they loaded up their guns and got ready.

"Hey, Sean, you, Lick, and Corey will be riding with me in the same car. All the rest of you, talk with each other and figure out who will be riding with who and do it quick because we do not have all day. We need to stick it to them now before they move out to somewhere else. Right now while we got the drop, we need to go and drop them very fast and then get the heck out of there. Hey, Worm, do not be acting all scary. Just handle business and move on to the next person. We need to get this over tonight. I want eight people in each SUV and I will ride in the middle since we are the strongest in our whole crew. If we are taken out then the team becomes weak."

The team moved out four SUVs deep plus Mike's car, which was in the middle as they drove to Big Rome's location. The whole time Jacob was calling Corey's phone but Corey was not picking up. Corey knew that Jacob would not do anything but try to talk him out of what he was doing.

Meanwhile, back at Big Rome's location, everyone was eating, drinking, and having a good time. They had strippers dancing while they were popping bottles and just having a ball celebrating Big Rome's little cousin's 30th birthday. They were well protected with heavy security and were in a place where they thought everything was good, so they were not expecting anything bad to happen.

*****

"This has just been a crazy day, Pastor Mark. I just want to go home and get some rest," Jacob told Pastor Mark.

"Well, Jacob, you know you can not just go home and get rest without praying for your family and friends. Let's go to the church and pray for a little while, then you can go home and get some rest," said Pastor Mark. As Pastor Mark and Jacob were walking up to the church, they noticed a homeless man sitting on the steps outside. The homeless man asked for help because he had not eaten in days and needed somewhere to stay. The church had a brand new mission home about a block away. Jacob and Pastor Mark invited the homeless man inside the church to minister to him. They fed him some leftovers that were in the kitchen.

"Thank you Jesus for this good food," said the homeless man after eating the nice hot meal they'd provided.

"Where are you from, sir?" Jacob asked the homeless man.

"I am from New Jersey. I lost everything when I was caught cheating on my wife. A few weeks later, she committed suicide by running herself off the highway while she was coming home from work. This was a year I can never forget. She died on September 5, 1979 and she had caused a crazy car accident that killed a few other people along with her. I was so guilty for what I had done and really believe in my heart this was all because of me. If I never would have cheated on my wife she would've never killed herself and caused the car crash that killed those other people," the man said.

As the homeless man was telling his story, Pastor Mark could see the anger on Jacob's face. Jacob looked at Pastor Mark and started to cry.

"Hey, young man, I felt so bad I started drinking and not going to work. I lost my job and at the same time I was hurt more because my wife was two months pregnant so I never got a chance to see my wife give birth to my unborn child," said the man.

"Sir, my father was one of the people killed in that car crash," Jacob told him.

"Yeah, Jacob never got to see his father because his father died in that same car crash while he was on his way to the hospital to see Jacob's mother give birth to him. He was Jacob Sr. and Jacob Jr. is who is sitting before you now," said Pastor Mark.

"Just look at my driver's license," Jacob said, showing the homeless man his license, which showed his birthdate, September 5, 1979.

The homeless man looked at the ID and then at Jacob with tears in his eyes. His heart was very heavy, and he felt horrible. He cried out to Jacob, asking him for his forgiveness.

"It's not about me, sir; it is about making it right with the Lord. See, you might have done the wrong thing back then but today you have the chance to make it right with Him and only you can make that decision. I forgive you because God forgives us all and if God can forgive me

147

then I should be able to forgive you. Are you ready to ask Jesus into your life today to be your savior?"

"Yes," the homeless man cried, "I am ready."

Pastor Mark and Jacob prayed with the man and he accepted Jesus Christ into his life. When he lifted his head, he was saved. After they talked for a little longer, they took the man to the mission home up the street. "What is your name, sir? We did not get your name," Jacob said.

"My name is Steve."

*****

Meanwhile, Mike and his team had finally pulled up at Big Rome's hangout spot. They circled around the block to scope out the place and see what position everyone was in before making their move on Big Rome and his crew.

"Hey, Lick, get out the car and look for any security that Big Rome may have surrounding the place," Mike ordered.

Lick got out of the car, grabbed a pistol from Corey, attached a silencer to it, and then went to scope the place out. Mike radioed some more of his goons on the walkie-talkie, telling them to get out of the SUV and back Lick up and check out the surroundings.

Lick walked around to the back of the spot and saw one of Big Rome's security guards. He took the guard out with a single headshot. As Lick and the other goons continued to check out the hangout spot, they spotted more of Big Rome's security guards and started to pick them off by killing them one by one.

Finally, Mike got the word that all of the security guards surrounding the building were taken out and that it was okay for the rest of the crew to start moving in.

"A'ight, people, I just got the word that we're all good to move in. Let's go inside in groups of three at a time to avoid looking shady doing it, because we need to make a grand entrance into this place. Big Rome does not expect this so now that we got the drop it's time that we take him out once and for all," said Mike.

Mike and his team started moving in three at a time, slowly creeping their way up to Big Rome's hangout spot to give him and his crew a nice surprise.

Chapter 10

THE SHOOTOUT

Matthew 26:52 KJV

Then said Jesus unto him put up again thy sword into his place: for all they that take the sword shall perish with the sword.

Mike and his goons finally made a special appearance in Big Rome's hangout spot. As Mike turned the corner, he saw a red dot on his black leather jacket.

"Hey, Mike, look out!" Corey screamed and pushed Mike out the way as shots were fired. Mike ran to the steps and hid behind a short wall for protection as he clapped his 40 caliber handgun. He hit one person with two slugs to the chest, putting him down. Lick was right above Mike, fighting with his bare hands. He threw the guy over the ledge above Mike and the guy landed on the floor right next to the same man that Mike had just laid down. Two men jumped out of a room with 9mm pistols and Corey shot one, putting him down, but missed the other man and they continued exchanging gunfire back and forth, neither getting a clear shot.

One of Mike's goons came from the other side and killed the guy that was shooting at Corey instantly with a

151

headshot. The man that Corey had laid down shot Mike's goon in the back and finished him off with a single shot to the face.

"Hey, let's move and spread out," said Mike. He was speaking to his team as if he was the general of an army. As shots continued to be fired back and forth by both parties, Corey's gun jammed and he was unable to shoot. Mike threw him his 40 caliber with the extended clip. Then Mike got an AK from one of his goons and started spitting and ripping everything, taking down at least 12 to 14 people from Big Rome's team.

Now that the room had been cleared, Mike wanted to look for Big Rome. Just as he looked up, a short man turned the corner and started shooting at him. Mike only had the AK with about eight rounds left and he was too close to use it to take the guy out. The man was still letting off shots and no one could get to him. As he came up from behind the short dude, Lick shot the man in the back of his legs, putting him down. Then Lick stood over him and shot him five times, ending him.

"Hey, look for Big Rome. Whoever finds him first, bring him to me and you will be paid a bonus and listed the top goon of the year," Mike said.

Everyone on Mike's team continued to shoot their way past the rest of Big Rome's. Out of nowhere, Big Rome finally appeared with four other men protecting him. Big Rome started to shoot at Mike and his team, hitting and killing some of them.

"What, you thought it was going to be real sweet, Mike? You got me messed up if you thought I was going out like that," said Big Rome. As Mike and Big Rome clapped shots at each other, more people on both teams were hurt or killed. The shootout continued until the police finally rushed into Big Rome's hangout spot.

"Freeze! Everyone put the guns down now!" A flash and smoke bomb was thrown, blinding everyone on both teams. Mike and Corey made their escape through the back door.

Mike was able to see through the smoke and spot Big Rome. He let off three shots, and one caught Big Rome right in the chest, putting him down on the ground immediately. Lick managed to exit from the top floor onto the roof and off the roof to the back exit from which Mike and Corey were making their escape. As the three of them pulled off, a few of Mike's, other goons managed to escape in one of the three SUVs that they came in.

"Someone get me an ambulance quick! There's people bleeding and injured all over the freaking place," said one of the police officers.

Finally, several ambulances arrived on the scene and the paramedics started helping people and putting them in the ambulances. Big Rome was bleeding out in the back of one of the ambulances as he was rushed to the emergency room. He was losing way too much blood. Several of Big Rome and Mike's goons died on the way to the hospital.

Back at Big Rome's spot there were at least 12 police detectives on the crime scene. They had the whole place taped off with yellow caution tape. There were bodies everywhere.

Meanwhile, Mike, Corey, and Lick were driving away from the crime scene, making their great escape from the law. They were discussing their next move and what they needed to do to finish off Big Rome if he did not die in the hospital.

"It is getting very crazy now. We all have to lay low because there were police everywhere. I am going back to Miami until things calm down a little because you know I am really still on the run, even with my new fake ID. I am still not trying to take any chances so I got to get the heck out of dodge. Before I go back to Miami I have to make sure that Big Rome is dead and out of the picture for good," said Mike.

Mike, Corey, and Lick went to Mike's laundromat office to set up another meeting. Mike called the rest of the goons that were left and got them to meet them at the laundromat to have a final meeting. Mike ordered pizza, buffalo wings, and beer for everyone to eat and drink, and while they were eating and drinking they discussed their next moves. As Mike talked to the team about how they would make their next moves and him laying low in Miami, Corey went to use the restroom. Lick was steady bragging and talking about how many bodies he'd laid down during the shootout, when Mike walked into the kitchen in the back of the laundromat and got his 40 caliber. Then he went back to the meeting room where his team was and he could still hear Lick loudly bragging about how many bodies he'd caught.

"Why are you going on and on about what we did earlier?" Mike asked Lick.

"Hey, man, we did our thing. You were nice spitting that AK at them jokers," said Lick. Mike reached behind him, pulled the 40 caliber from his waistband, and shot Lick right in the head, killing him dead on the spot. Everyone was looking at Mike as if he had lost his mind.

"You see, when you do things with me it is never good. The moves you make with me lead you to the grave or to jail. Whenever we make a move, whether it involves getting money or killing people, never speak on it again after it is done because you never know who may be listening or watching. Eyes and ears are everything and one spoken word can get you dead or behind bars for the rest of your life. You see Lick, who is laying here bleeding out the head now, he always ran his mouth like a chick and I wanted to give him the benefit of the doubt because he never talked about what we did around me before. I would always just hear from other people about him running his mouth so I never tripped. Lick's talking, bragging, and running his mouth made him a major liability because he put everyone standing here in a bad place. So do not sit here looking at me like I am the bad guy because I just saved us a whole bad issue we could've had come down the pipeline. Where is Corey?" said Mike.

"In the rest room," one of Mike's goons let him know. Corey was in the restroom and very scared and nervous after hearing Mike's 40 caliber going off. He

155

knew that he had shot someone. Corey had called Jacob immediately for help because he knew how Mike got when he blacked out. He would take out his frustration out on anyone, especially someone who did something that he thought made him look weak.

When Corey called Jacob and let him know what happened, his advice to Corey was to leave immediately. Corey exited the laundromat by climbing out of a window, driving off and leaving the rest of the team with Mike. Corey drove to meet Jacob at his house but he was not there. He called him but got no answer so he called Latasha.

"Hey, babe, I need to get out of town real quick because a lot of drama just went down and I can't talk about it over the phone. Just know we need to meet up ASAP," said Corey.

"Okay, let's meet at our old school in the back parking lot and we can just leave your car there and I will drive us to somewhere safe and out of sight from everyone," said Latasha.

Corey called Jacob again and still got no answer so he left a voice message on his phone to let him know that he was safe with Latasha, and that he is going out of town for a little while to let things cool down. He said he would fill him in with the details later, whenever they spoke or met up. He told Jacob to tell Hannah he said hello and to get better soon.

*****

Jacob and Pastor Mark were back at the hospital to see Hannah. They wanted to check on her to see if she was making progress so she could come home. As Pastor Mark and Jacob walked into the hospital, they see Hector Martez's name on the door of a room that was only four rooms down the hall from Hannah's room. Hector Martez was Big Rome's real name so Pastor Mark asked Jacob to peek into the room to see if it was Big Rome. Pastor Mark knew that if Big Rome saw him he would know or think that he still had a connection with Mike. Jacob went into Big Rome's room but no one was in the bed. Jacob knocked on the bathroom door inside Big Rome's room and no one answered so he opened the door but there was no one in the bathroom. It appeared that Big Rome had gotten up and left the hospital.

Jacob brought the news back to Pastor Mark as they headed to Hannah's room. When they entered her room, she was watching the news. The reporter was talking about the big shootout and stated that 16 people were dead and four were seriously injured. After the news went off Hannah gave them the good news that she would be able to come home from the hospital in the morning. Then she asked Jacob to bring her purse over and she reached in and pulled out a nice shiny diamond ring and handed it to him.

"Your father gave this ring to me when he asked me to marry him, son. Now I want to give you this same ring for you to give to Lisa and ask her the same question," Hannah told her son.

"Wow, Mom, this ring is nice. It looks very expensive. And Dad gave this to you? I can not accept

157

this ring from you, Mom. I'd rather save up money and buy Lisa a new ring when the time is right," said Jacob.

"Like heck you will, son. Not now. You will take this ring and you will use it to propose to Lisa. Why spend the money, which would be a few thousand dollars, when you can just use this ring free of charge and save money?" said Hannah. After Pastor Mark spoke some sense into Jacob, he finally decided to take the ring from Hannah.

Jacob asked Hannah about somewhere nice he could take Lisa to pop the question to her, and Hannah gave Jacob the location of the place where Jacob Sr. asked her to marry him. After they finished coming up with the plans for what they would do, they said a prayer for Hannah to sleep well. They stayed and talked to Hannah for another couple of hours and then they left the hospital for the day. On the way out Jacob looked into Big Rome's room again and saw that he was not there.

*****

Back at Mike's laundromat, after removing Lick's dead body and cleaning up his blood from the floor, everyone was listening to Mike speak about his new moves. Suddenly, the door is kicked in and almost 30 cops come running into the laundromat. They had received a tip from someone about the location of Mike's new spot.

"Everyone get down on the ground now!" an officer yelled as more police continued to rush their way into the laundromat. Gunshots sounded as Mike's team engaged in a shootout with the police. Mike's goons were going down as they were hit. Mike was blasting while running toward the exit. He knew that there were way too many police and all he could see was jail before his eyes, so he continued to blast his way out to a back door and ran down into the basement and then through another door leading him into the small candy store that was next door to his laundromat. It turned out that the candy store that was next to his was also his store but registered under Latasha's mother's name. Mike managed to make a clean getaway by going through his candy store. Meanwhile, all the other goons on Mike's team were killed in gun battle with the police. Two of the police officers were killed as well and died right on the scene.

Mike drove off in his car and jumped right on the highway to head straight to Miami. While Mike drove, he called Corey's phone but Corey did not pick up. Mike started to become very suspicious, thinking maybe Corey was the one who tipped off the police to come and raid the place. He already knew how close he was getting to Lick before he shot him dead.

Corey saw the call coming in but he refused to answer the phone as he was very upset about what Mike had done to his boy Lick. Corey spoke with Latasha and told her everything that he was involved in with her father and how the police had raided the place.

"Hey, babe, I do not know for sure but your pop may think I told the law on him," said Corey.

"Why would you say a thing like that, Corey? What would make you even think that? My dad really likes you and looks at you like a son," said Latasha.

"Well, your dad just killed Lick by shooting him right in the head."

"What? He shot Lick? Why did he do that?"

"Lick was running his mouth about today's events and your pop thought that he would have been a liability, and he said he could not have that. He said that whatever we did is done and there is no need to talk about it again. I am here now with you to let you know if something happens to me then your dad or Big Rome may have something to do with me being gone."

"Do not say that, Corey. You are really starting to scare me and I am starting to not know what to do. We need to call Jacob up so that he can pray with us."

"No, I do not want to call Jacob up right now because he is having issues of his own. Let's just let the night go by and then we will call everyone to meet up in the morning."

*****

As the next day came Corey and Latasha were hiding out in a hotel and staying low because of the drama with Corey and Mike, the big shootout with Big Rome and Mike, and then the raid by police a few hours later. Corey had been involved in too much drama and it was starting to hurt him. Latasha had room service deliver breakfast to their room at the hotel they were crashing at. After they both ate breakfast, Corey called Jacob to let him know what had happened last night and Jacob wanted to finally meet up to tell him what he and Pastor Mark had seen at the hospital.

Finally, Jacob met Corey at the hotel that he and Latasha were staying at. He told Corey that he had been visiting his mom when he found out that Big Rome had left the hospital.

"Man, what happened to Big Rome? When I walked past the room Pastor Mark told me that was Big Rome laid up in the room. He sent me into the room since Big Rome doesn't know me; he just saw me in the mall that one time when we were all together. When I checked in the room, there was a lot of blood everywhere but he was not in the room. I knocked on the bathroom door and no one answered. After we left the hospital, we checked his room one last time on our way out," said Jacob to Corey.

"Man, last night was crazy drama. We got into a big shootout with Big Rome's crew. Mike had the drop on the spot where Big Rome and his goons were chilling. We took out all of his security first and then made our way into the hangout spot. They did not expect us at all. Police later burst into Big Rome's spot and then everyone was trying to run out to avoid going to jail. I was jumping and stepping all over dead bodies and Mike managed to escape as well. Later, after we all got back to Mike's laundromat, everyone was eating pizza and drinking beer. I started to think that Mike was not very happy about something because I had seen that look in his eyes before. I went into the bathroom and that is when I called you. Right after I was done speaking to you, I found out that Lick was shot by Mike. Mike had shot Lick right in the head and left him on the floor dead," said Corey as he told Jacob about the drama that had happened last night.

"Why did Mike shoot Lick and how did you manage to get out of the laundromat?"

"I heard Mike saying the reason why he shot Lick was because he was running his mouth and now he could be a liability. I managed to get out of the window that was in the restroom. Now I think Mike will be coming for me because I disappeared and then the police raided the place."

"So you believe that Mike is thinking you ratted on him now?"

"Yes, I believe he would be thinking that I called the police on him because he knew how I was cool with Lick. He may think that I was mad at him for killing Lick and wanted to get even with him by calling the Law. Lick was cool and I still feel some type of way but Mike is like my father-in-law just because of Latasha," said Corey.

"Well, if you do what I am about to do with Lisa then you do not have to worry about Mike coming back and killing you," said Jacob as he laughs at Corey.

"What you mean Jacob? What are you about to do?"

"I am about to pop the question to Lisa and ask her to marry me before we go back to school. Check this out, bro." Jacob pulled the ring out of his pocket and showed Corey, sneakily, so that Latasha could not see.

"Man, this ring is sick. Where did you get it?"

"It was my mom dukes'. She got it from my dad when he asked her to marry her."

"Yeah, bro, Lisa is going to like this. These diamonds are official, yo."

"Yeah, my mom and I had a few long talks and she told me to go for it. You know how my mom dukes does. She wants things to be in God's order."

"Yeah, bro, you never lied about that. But in the meantime, what you think I need to do?" Corey asked.

"First you need to get things patched up with Mike and then get yourself ready for school. Every time you get around Mike you get caught up in the drama, Corey. You need to learn to make more Godly decisions because one wrong decision can have you dead or in jail for the rest of your life. When are you going to see that God keeps showing you mercy in your life? The devil keeps trying to pull me into the things of the world but I had to realize that God is much greater. I am not going to keep trying to impress people. The only one I need to impress is God. You just need to pray and ask Jesus to come into your life for real this time, Corey. You can not keep killing and think nothing is going to happen to you. Ask yourself, who do you think you are taking someone else's life? You have no right to take a life because you did not give life. There is only one person who has the right to do that and that's God. It is very sad to say and I am not speaking death into your life, but if you do not repent for your sins God will take the breath from you, Corey. I love you and you are

163

like my brother, but I cannot make you fully accept Jesus because it has to be a choice that you make for yourself. Sometimes I do not know who you are anymore. I never know which Corey I will get. Some days I pray and hope that you never pull a gun out on me and shoot me down dead. You have to get back into the things of God, brother, because he has a purpose for you," said Jacob, as he honestly and wholeheartedly ministered to Corey.

Finally, everyone linked up to meet Hannah at the hospital because she was ready to check out and go home. Hannah spoke with the doctor and he stated that her stomach cancer seemed to be going away from what he could see on the last scan they'd done. The doctor stated that it looked like some kind of miracle. Hannah told the doctor that she serves a mighty God who makes miracles all day and every day in different people's lives. The doctor decided to give his life to Jesus Christ because it was something that he'd never seen in his life before.

*****

Later on that day, after Hannah was taken home from the hospital everyone went out to dinner. While waiting at dinner everyone was watching one of the TVs that was on in the restaurant and saw Mike's mugshot on the screen. The news had said that Mike was wanted for questioning for the major shootout that had taken place last night.

Meanwhile, Jacob had already had a meeting with Lisa's parents to ask for her hand and Lisa's parents told Jacob that the both of them could not be happier. Finally, while everyone was eating, Jacob asked Lisa to stand and then he grabbed her hand and asked her if she would be his wife.

"Yes, Jacob, I would love to be your wife!" she said with joy. Jacob pulled out the ring that his mother gave him and Lisa was stunned. As Jacob placed the ring on Lisa's finger she was extremely excited. "Watch out, everyone. Mrs. Justice is coming," Lisa laughed. Jacob thought he saw a hint of envy on Latasha's face as she looked at Lisa. When she hugged Lisa, it did not seem genuine.

As everyone continued to eat, Corey also clearly saw the jealous look on Latasha's face. "Don't worry," he leaned over and said to her, "I will be asking you the same question soon. First, I need to speak with your father and then we can move on from there."

They were all very happy for Lisa and Jacob, and Hannah had already begun speaking about the things that needed to be done for planning the wedding. The two planned to get married in the next 15 months because they wanted to have enough time to save up their money and have the nice wedding that Lisa dreamed of. In addition, Jacob wanted Lisa to be almost finished college and settled in. He was also thinking about doubling his classes and taking some summer classes to finish with his Master's Degree. Pastor Mark offered Jacob a job at the church as an associate pastor for the rest of the summer. Jacob knew that it would be a great opportunity for him to earn some extra money so he accepted Pastor Mark's offer.

As everyone was leaving the restaurant, a police detective by the name of Jason Shan grabbed Corey up and asked him to take a ride down to the police station with him.

"Hey, bro, call my mom and tell her I am locked up and I may need bail money," said Corey to Jacob.

"Why would you need bail money, Mr. Corey?" Detective Shan laughed. "You are starting to sound guilty already and I haven't even asked you one question yet. Man, get the heck in this car and take this ride downtown. All I know is that your answers to these questions we ask you better be on point, because if we get any clue that you're telling us lies we will keep you. You don't get bail for murder, Corey, so play with me if you want." Everyone watched as Corey rode off in the detective's car.

"Man, this is crazy. If it's not one thing it's always another," Jacob said, very upset.

"Just have faith, young brother, because everything happens for a reason. This may be Corey's way of learning. Maybe now he will allow Jesus to fully come into his life and he can learn to walk in the full will of God and not hang with the wrong people. God never makes mistakes. He knows the best way to reach Corey and that is by allowing him to take the trip downtown, so do not stress because everything happens in God's order," said Pastor Mark.

Chapter 11

TURN FROM YOUR WICKED WAYS

2 Chronicles 7:14 KJV

If my people, which are called by my name, shall humble themselves, and pray, and seek my face, and turn from their wicked ways; then will I hear from heaven, and will forgive their sin, and will heal their land.

Jacob's phone rang and it was Corey's mother on the line. She wanted to know what happened and why the police came and took Corey downtown. After Jacob told her what happened he asked her if she could meet him at a place where they could talk in person because he did not want to talk about some things over the phone. Finally, Jacob met with Corey's mother and let her know everything that Corey was involved in. He knew in his mind and deep down that it was right telling her everything. Jacob felt that it was for Corey's own good.

Back at the police station, Detective Shan was asking Corey all types of questions about Mike and all the other murders that he may have been connected to.

"Look, man, I do not know what you're talking about. I don't have the answers to any of these questions you're asking me.

"So where were you last night, Corey? I was over my girl's house watching a movie."

"So, if I call your girl right now would she be able to say the same thing you just told me?"

"Heck yeah, she would, but let me ask you, am I under arrest? If I am not under arrest you might as well let me know because I do not know what you're talking about. You are talking to the moon, my dude, because you are not going to sit here and try to make me tell you something that I do not know about. If you're not locking me up and taking me to my cell then let me go. You are wasting my time. I do not know anything."

"Well, Corey, I think you do and just for that you will be spending your night right here."

"Look, I need to speak to my lawyer before you lock me up."

"You know what, Corey, I am going to let you go, so don't even worry about contacting your lawyer. You are just as dead on the streets anyway."

Detective Shan let Corey go and sent him on his way. As soon as Corey was free, he called his mother and then called Latasha to let them both know that everything was good. He then called Jacob to let him know everything that Detective Shan was asking him.

Back inside the police station, Detective Shan's phone rang. "What's up, my man? Everything is good with me on my end. What about you?"

"I'm good, my man. How did Corey do when you questioned him? Did he rat or stand tall? Did he say my name and tell you everything that went down?" Mike asked the detective.

It turned out that Mike and Detective Jason Shan were very cool with one another. The detective was on Mike's payroll and he helped get things cleared away from Mike whenever trouble with the law came.

"I need you to keep a close eye on Corey because he can be a liability and you know I do not get down with that. If he starts to be a problem, I might have to lay him down and I do not care if he is dating my daughter or not. I can not go to jail, you feel me, man?" Mike said.

"Yeah, I feel you Mike. I don't think Corey will be any trouble, but I'll still keep a close watch on him to see if he starts to slip up. I will come visit you next week to get my money from you."

"Come on, Jason, don't even come at me like that. You know I'm going to fatten your pockets right up."

*****

The next morning was Sunday and Pastor Mark asked Jacob if he could preach the word. When Hannah and Jacob arrived at the church they saw Steve, the homeless man who Jacob and Pastor Mark had led to

Christ.   Jacob never told his mother what he'd learned about Steve's involvement in his father's death. He didn't want to upset her.

As Jacob walked to the pulpit, the worship team was on fire and had everyone in the church hyped up with their inspirational words.   After the praise and worship team was done worshiping, Jacob walked up and read a scripture out of his Holy Bible. It was from 2 Chronicles 7:14 which reads, *If my people, which are called by my name, shall humble themselves, and pray, and seek my face, and turn from their wicked ways; then will I hear from heaven, and will forgive their sin, and will heal their land.*

"Today I want to speak about the choices that we all make in life. The title of this message is *Are you really a child of God?* Today many of us walk around talking about we are children of God but when we are not around saved people we act like we sinners.   It is time for us to stop playing church and be real with the Lord, because He sees everything.   Some of you are sleeping around and telling yourself that since no one from the church can see you, you are good.   You're quick to impress people but not to impress God. You see, the people may not see you but God does.   That is why you have to really give your life to Jesus. You have to know that Jesus Christ is Lord and that He can save you from anything. God can never use you unless you fully give your life to Him. God wants people that He can use and raise up to go out and win other lost souls to this Gospel. How can He use you if you're out sinning repeatedly? You are no better than the sinner that you are trying to win over. It is time to shine light on the lost souls. Be faithful and real with the Lord so when a sinner looks at you they can see the light."

As Jacob continued to preach the Word, the church doors opened and a small ray of light peeked through the crack between the doors.

A man started walking into the church and as the man came through the doors Jacob could see that it was Big Rome. He sat down in the back of the church and when Corey looked up and saw him he was in shock. As Jacob continued to preach the Word of God, Big Rome started coming straight for Corey. He pulled out a gun and pointed it at Corey.

"You see, today is the day of salvation for you, Hector Martez. Yeah, that's right, you are about to be filled with the Holy Spirit today. After today, you will surrender your life to Jesus and shall never touch a gun again," Jacob said.

Big Rome turned his attention from Corey to Jacob, now pointing the gun at Jacob instead.

"I declare and decree in the name of Jesus for you, Hector, to put down that gun and ask Jesus to come in your life," Jacob preached to Big Rome.

Everyone in the church was looking at Jacob like he was crazy but Jacob did not pay them any mind because he was in the Spirit and he'd seen the face of Jesus and an image of his father that made him feel safe. Corey ran to Pastor Mark and whispered in his ear, telling him to make it stop before Jacob was killed. Big Rome was debating in his mind, trying to decide whether he should shoot Jacob or just drop the gun. He felt like the Lord was starting to take over his mind and make him have second thoughts about shooting Jacob. Jacob looked over to the praise and worship team and then at the congregation. People were in shock and some had their phones out, taking pictures and filming video footage. He looked back over at the praise and worship team and gestured for them to begin singing as he spoke.

"Hey, Big Rome, if you're going to shoot me then go ahead and shoot me because I know where I will be afterwards. I will be absent from my body but I will be with the Lord. Hallelujah! You see, your gun does not scare me because God is greater. Today can be your day for salvation if you just allow Jesus Christ to come into your life. Let me ask you something, Big Rome. If you were to die today do you know where you would spend eternity? I know where I will be but where you will be? It is time to put down your gun and give your life over to the Lord. Jesus loves you and I love you. I want nothing more for you than for you to give your life to the Lord. Every knee shall bow and every tongue shall confess that Jesus Christ is Lord. You have a choice. You can choose life or death, and today is your time to choose," said Jacob as he continued to minister to Big Rome.

As Big Rome looked up, tears could be seen in his eyes and it looked like peace was falling on him.

"Hector Martez, it is time for you to give your life to the Lord and leave Big Rome behind you. God showed you mercy way too many times when you could have been dead. It is time to give your life to Jesus Christ today and move into victory."

Big Rome dropped the gun and fell onto his knees, crying out to the Lord with a heavy burden on him. Jacob came closer to Big Rome and put his right hand on his shoulder and asked him to repeat the prayer unto the Lord.

"Dear Jesus, I ask that you forgive me for all my sins. I know that I am a sinner but I no longer want to be a sinner. I ask that you please come into my life and take over. Allow your Holy Spirt to come upon me and give me the power to fight the devil when he tries to stop me from living for you. I do believe that you died on the cross and then rose from the dead. I want to give it all to you today and just ask that all my sins are forgiven. In Jesus' name, amen."

After Big Rome gave his life, he gave Jacob a big hug. "Thank you for saving my life." Pastor Mark asked the church security to pick up the gun that Big Rome had dropped on the floor of the church. Then he walked up to Big Rome and apologized for what he had done to him alongside Mike years ago. He explained to Big Rome that it was the old him who had done that, and that he was renewed by Christ and now happy to be on the same team fighting against the devil together.

Jacob called the people from the church congregation to come and greet their new brother in Christ, welcoming him into the church. "You see, this is what it is all about; winning lost souls over to Jesus Christ. It is not about me, it is not about Pastor Mark, and not about any of you. It is all about Jesus Christ, the Lord of our Salvation. We are tools used by God to bring souls in for His Glory. If it was up to us we would have all been somewhere dead, but God spared our lives," said Jacob to the church congregation.

When church service was over Hannah came over to give her son a hug and tell him how proud she was for how he had allowed God to use him.

"Thanks, Mom, but you know there are still many lost souls out here that need to be saved and they may not have tomorrow because today can be their last day. That includes Mike," said Jacob.

As Hector was talking to Pastor Mark about old times, he began to feel very bad about trashing the church. He reached into his pockets and pulled out all the money that was in them; it was $9,000. He promised Pastor Mark that he would bless him with more money in a week or so.

"You see, Hector, I told you God is greater than you are."

"Yes, you did, but now I have to go back and tell the rest of the team not to come after you," said Hector.

"What about Mike? What will you do for him?"

"I will do nothing but let the goons deal with him. You get a pass because you didn't pull the trigger. I was only going to kill you because you were with him when he left me for dead," said Hector.

"I understand what you're saying and where you're coming from, Hector, but you have to leave the battle to the

Lord because God said *vengeance is mine.* You are now a servant of God and you need to do what pleases Him."

"You're right. I will call the goons off him as well to keep the peace. But what about me? You know Mike will still be after me if he finds out that I am still alive. How will I know if he will chill and leave me be? He will try to kill me if he sees me. How can I protect myself from Mike?"

"You still have goons that work for you, Hector. Just have four of them guard you the same as they did before, but now you can start working on them leading them to Jesus Christ."

"Okay, I will start with that and I will see you on Thursday night for Bible study," said Hector.

"That is what I like to hear. Look how God does. He is awesome!"

As everyone was leaving the church, Corey looked across the street from the church and saw Detective Shan's car parked. The window rolled down.

"What's up, Corey? How was church service?" he asked, and then pulled off, laughing. Detective Shan called Mike and let him know Big Rome had been inside Pastor Mark's church.

"You see, I knew something was not right with Mark. That dude continues to cross me. He was like my brother but it is time we take Mark out along with Big

175

Rome. When all the heat calms down I am going to blow Mark's double-crossing, backstabbing head off!"

"Mike, I know you wanted Big Rome dead and I can understand that, but are you sure that you want to kill a pastor?"

"Heck yeah! He's no pastor in my eyes. He's just Mark to me. I know him."

"Well, my man, you are on your own with that. I will not be helping you."

"Oh, Jason, you will help me because if you don't, I have all the work that you helped me do documented and recorded and I will send the proof over to your captain and to Internal Affairs. This will prove that you were an accessory to murder and you will be locked up behind bars. You know what happens to a cop who ends up behind bars, right? All the people that you helped put away will be trying to kill you every day in jail."

"Mike, are you trying to threaten me?"

"Oh no, man. It is not a threat; it is a promise. So do your job and you will be good. You will not have to worry about me. You will be able to keep getting money and live well without any problems," said Mike.

"Whatever, man, just pay me my money and I will come up with a plan to take out Pastor Mark. Once I help you with this last plan, our business is done. You will have to do everything on your own from then on. My fee for this service is $10,000 since this is a pastor we're talking about instead of a normal street thug."

"Alright, I will pay you. You just need to make sure you hold up your end of the bargain and I will hold up my end. We will talk in three days, Jason, and remember, I need this to be very neat. Do not screw this up."

"Whatever, man, I got this. Just come up with the cash. Peace." Detective Shan hung up the phone with Mike and headed back downtown to the station to pull Pastor Mark's record up to see how he could frame him or set him up to be murdered.

Jacob, Hannah, Pastor Mark, and Hector all met up the next day to fellowship and have lunch. As they were eating their lunch, Hector gave everyone the heads up and told Pastor Mark to watch his back because he had gotten news from a very reliable source and that Mike was working with someone from the police department.

"You are my brother in Christ now and I still got all ears to the street so I give you the news, Pastor," said Hector.

"Thank you, Hector. Good looking out for the drop but remember God is greater than Mike and his tricks," Pastor Mark replied.

As everyone was outside waiting to get the cars back from the valet, two black cars crept up slowly and fired shots.

"Get down now!" Jacob pushed Hannah inside the lunch buffet and jumped inside after her as shots rang out. People were running everywhere and Big Rome was being hit. Pastor Mark was laying on the ground next to Big Rome and they both had blood all over of them. A man stepped out of one of the cars and stood over Big Rome, firing more shots into him to finish him off. The man stood over Pastor Mark next and tried to shoot him, but the gun jammed up. He got back in the car and the two cars sped off. Someone inside the lunch buffet had called 911 so the boys in blue were already on their way.

"Hang in there, brother, do not die on me. Fight, come on, fight!" Pastor Mark said to Hector.

"Hey, Pastor, tell Jacob I said thank you for allowing God to use him to lead me to Jesus Christ."

"No, man, you going to be fine. Just hang on. Come on, the ambulance is on the way. Just hang in there a little longer."

The ambulance got to the lunch buffet and a crowd had gathered so it was hard for the paramedics to get through.

"Move, everyone! Clear it out for us. We need room to do our job!" one of the paramedics screamed out to all the people. Finally, they got through and were able to pick Hector up and lay him on the stretcher. They put an IV in his right arm and put an oxygen mask on his face to help him breathe. Pastor Mark got inside the back of the ambulance with Hector as they drove to the nearest hospital. Jacob and Hannah drove in Jacob's car to the hospital.

Just three minutes before Hector got to the hospital, he died. Pastor Mark just sat in the back of the ambulance grieving. He was not grieving for the fact that Hector was dead; he was just thinking about the last days in which we are living. Pastor Mark was crying for the souls that are lost for he knew that they would not see the kingdom of heaven if they did not give their lives to Jesus Christ.

When Jacob and Hannah pulled up to the hospital, they saw Pastor Mark crying with blood all over his clothes and then they saw the paramedics putting Hector in a body bag.

As Pastor Mark got into the back of Jacob's car, one of the paramedics came over and handed Pastor Mark a piece of paper that was folded up in Hector's wallet. It was a letter that Hector had written three hours before they'd gone out for lunch. The letter read:

To my new church family,

I put this letter inside my wallet to let you know not to mourn for me if I die because I am in the glory of the Lord. Pastor Mark, I made plans for something to be sent to the church in the event of my death. So if you are reading this short letter, just expect something to show up at the church with in the next three to four business days.

Hector

"Wow, this is crazy and way too much for me to deal with today. I cannot believe this all happened in broad daylight," Jacob said.

"Jacob, before Hector died he told me to tell you he said thank you for allowing God to use you to lead him to Jesus Christ," said Pastor Mark.

Jacob dropped Pastor Mark off at his house and called some of the church security to take different shifts to keep Pastor Mark safe. It was very clear that Mike had it out for Pastor Mark just as well as he had it out for Hector. Jacob got a call from Corey and Corey told him that Big Rome had died. Jacob said that he knew because he was there. Then he told Corey that he did not want to talk now and just wanted to get his mother home safe.

While driving Hannah home, Jacob started to think very hard to himself. How did Corey know about Hector dying? He started to put the piece of the puzzle together. *It was Corey that called the hit!* He dropped Hannah off at his house and then called Corey back but he did not pick up his phone. Jacob left a voice message on his phone telling him to call back because it was very important.

Jacob began to pray in his car, crying out to God. "Why, God, why? You used me to win him over for your glory. Why did you take him that fast? He did not have a chance to live a good life for a whole week before you took him. Why is Corey turning into a devil? He loved you and it is not like him to be doing these evil things to people. It is as if I do not even know him as my friend anymore. I am asking you for understanding in all of this. Please show me a sign. Why is all this drama happening? When will all this really go away? When will peace come for good?"

Jacob then tried calling Corey's phone again and still he got no answer. Jacob drove to Lisa's house and found her crying and very upset.

"Hey, what's wrong, babe? What's going on? What happened?" he asked her.

"It's Latasha. She was found two hours ago with her throat cut from ear to ear. A witness is down at the police station trying to identify the man who is responsible. It was someone from Big Rome's crew who did it because Mike called the hit on Big Rome and had him killed. They wanted to even the score," Lisa cried.

"How do you know all this? Who told you that?"

"They left a note right next to her dead body in Manchester Park, where she was found." Lisa's phone was steady ringing and Jacob asked her if she was going to pick up the phone. She said she wasn't going to because it was Corey and all he was going to ask was where Latasha was.

"What can I tell him? I don't want to be the one to tell him that Latasha is dead." Jacob looked at Lisa's phone and saw that there were four missed calls from Corey.

Jacob called Corey from his own phone and Corey still did not pick up. "Hey, Lisa, you need to call Corey back because he is not picking up his phone when I call him."

"Why would he not pick up his phone for you? That is not like him."

"Lisa, I have something to tell you and you have to relax and not get upset when I tell you this. I believe Latasha is dead because of Corey."

"What do you mean and why would that be so?"

"Well, I think Corey is the one who called the hit on Big Rome and when Big Rome's goons found out, they took Latasha out to get back at Mike."

"This drama is starting to get crazier and crazier," said Lisa.

"I need you to call Corey to find out where he is so I can track him down," Jacob said.

Lisa called Corey and he answered the phone. "Hey, Lisa, where my babe at? I've been trying to reach her for the last four hours," said Corey.

"Corey, there is something I have to tell you but I do not want to tell you over the phone so where are you?" Lisa asked.

"I am downtown. I will come to you and should be there in 25 minutes," Corey said.

Jacob knew that even though he was a man of God, he would need to strap up. Corey had been acting very shady for the past two weeks and he did not know which Corey he would be getting.

"Lisa, I need you to go in your room under the big black chair and bring me my gun," Jacob told her.

"You know I do not like touching that thing. You go and get it yourself."

"Okay. Where are your parents? It may get messy."

"They are both out of town on business with their jobs."

Jacob went into Lisa's room and grabbed his 9mm pistol that he'd taken from the bag of guns they'd delivered to Light-skinned Chris a few years ago. He strapped himself up and waited for Corey in Lisa's living room while he made Lisa sit and wait outside on the steps.

Corey pulled up in front of Lisa's house and Lisa broke the news to him that Latasha was dead. Corey fell right down on ground, crying heavily with so much pain in his heart. Lisa grabbed him up off of the ground with a hug as she cried with him. Jacob was looking outside through Lisa's living room window. He was crying right along with them but knew it wasn't the right time to come outside yet. He needed to let the two of them get themselves together and he needed to do the same.

After over an hour of crying and grieving, Jacob came out of Lisa's house. "Hey, Corey, what is up? Why didn't you answer or return any of my phone calls?"

"My phone was dead," Corey said, lying right to Jacob's face.

"Well, your phone sure wasn't dead when Lisa called and, as a matter of fact, I called you when I was standing right next to her no more than a minute before she called you."

"So what are you trying to say, Jacob? Get to your point."

"I think I've made my point and let you know that I know what you did."

"What are you talking about? What did I do?"

"You know what you did, Corey. It was you the whole time. It wasn't Mike. *You* called the hit on Big Rome and had him gunned down in cold blood!"

"So what if I did? What, you're friends with the enemy now? That man killed my little sister and was still walking around breathing like everything was good. You might have accepted him as your new brother in Christ but not me. Did you think just because Big Rome gave his life to Jesus Christ that everything was going to change and he would have a good life? I mean, if I didn't get him, Mike would've gotten him soon anyway."

"Corey, Jesus Christ believes in giving people mercy, and you of all people should know that. However, while you're sitting here with your chest up acting like you're some kind of commando, you killed your own girlfriend. Yeah, that's right. You see, when you called the hit on Big Rome, one of his goons got the drop on Latasha after doing their homework and finding out that she is Mike's daughter. It is just as I always tried to tell you before; you have to make the smart decision, not allow the devil to trap you. That is exactly what happened. The devil tricked you into getting your own girlfriend killed," Jacob said.

"And, Corey, there is something else that you need to know," said Lisa. "Latasha was one month pregnant with your baby. She was going to tell you the news today."

Corey rushed at Jacob, trying to hurt him because of the truth that he had heard. Jacob pulled his gun out and cracked Corey right on the head with it. He hit him just hard enough to calm him down and put a small lump on the top of his head.

"What you going to do, preacher boy? You're not about that life. Make me a believer that you're going to use that gun." Jacob clapped two shots in the air while Corey was laying on the ground.

"You are not worth it. I will not allow the devil to come and cause corruption in my life. I will pray for you, Corey. I will pray that you come from your wicked ways before it is too late," said Jacob.

"You know this changes everything between us, Jacob. We are no longer brothers," Corey told him.

"I'd rather stand for Jesus Christ than to live with you in darkness, Corey."

Corey got up from the ground, got into his car, and drove off. Lisa hugged Jacob. She was traumatized after everything that had happened, especially losing her best friend. Jacob took her inside the house, made her some tea, and just held her as he prayed unto the Lord.

Chapter 12

JESUS IS THE LIGHT OF MY SALVATION

John 14:6 KJV

Jesus saith unto him, I am the way, the truth, and the life: no man cometh unto the Father, but by me.

The next day Jacob woke up with his heart very heavy knowing that two people were killed yesterday. Corey had told Mike the news about Latasha being murdered by one of Big Rome's goons. He immediately made a call to Detective Shan to order a hit on the guy who was responsible for killing Latasha because the police already had evidence pointing to him and they were holding him until his trial. Detective Shan called in a favor and had the man who killed Latasha whacked while his was eating breakfast. Detective Shan called Mike to let him know that the job was done and to talk about their plans for Pastor Mark.

"Hey, you know what, Jason? I will take care of Pastor Mark because it is more personal between the two of us. You can keep the money that I already paid you and that will be my payment for what you just took care of for me. I will be in town within the next few days to handle that joker Mark. In the meantime, check on Corey and tell him to call me from the burn out phone that I gave him," said Mike.

Detective Shan called Corey to deliver the message from Mike. Then he raced downtown to put in his two-week notice to quit the police force. He had been a corrupt cop for his entire career in the police force and had made over $4.5 million. He did everything from stealing drugs and guns from the evidence room in the police station to taking payoffs from well-known drug dealers. He knew that his luck would run out one day so he wanted to move out of the country. He had family and close friends living in the UK so his plan was to go there and stay for good.

Corey called Mike back after receiving the message from Detective Shan. "Good work, li'l homie. That is what I'm talking about. You get the top goon of the year award. Now I need you to make a few runs for me and meet in Miami. I know you're hurt about Latasha but we have to move on and handle a few things, then we will be all set. I will make you a rich man and you will not have to walk around with so much pain," said Mike.

"Yeah, but what else is there to do? You already took care of the person who killed Latasha. Big Rome is dead; I took care of that. So what else is there to do?" Corey asked.

"We have to handle Detective Shan and Mark."

"Are you talking about Pastor Mark?" Corey asked.

"Yes, Mark has to go just because he was always in my way when I tried to take care of business. I was trying to get Jacob down with me as you are now but Mark shielded him from doing that."

"I thought you and Pastor Mark were like brothers and always had each others' backs."

"We used to be like brothers but now since he turned holy he tries to act like I am the scum of the earth. I need you to take care of Detective Shan by putting him down and taking his money. I got the drop on that fool and heard that he is going to get his money and leave the country. You must stop him before he leaves and put an end to that shady cop."

"How would I do that? How would I even get close enough to take him out?"

"Everything is planned out for you and you will be able to touch him very easily. We have a nice car for you to drive and you will wait until he comes out of the bank with his money. Once he drives off you will tail him. Do not tail him so closely that he will notice that you are following him. Once he is at a red light where no one is around, hop out on him at the light and jump in his car, then blast that fool. Leave him dead inside the car and then drive his car to the location that I give you. I will have Spoon ride with you and he will drive your car while you drive Jason's car."

"I think it's a good plan, Mike, and I will take care of everything. I promise we will get Jason out of here because I never liked him anyway. I've been waiting to do him in for a long time now because I do not like shady cops," Corey said.

"I may have a little problem to handle later on but I will let you know," said Mike to Corey.

Corey knew deep down that it was Jacob Mike was talking about, however, he still saw Jacob as his brother and would not want to cause him any real harm. To avoid hurting Jacob, he decided to stay away from him.

*****

Jacob left Lisa's house and drove over to Pastor Mark's house. Hannah met them over there and they set up the funeral arrangements for Hector. Pastor Mark had been speaking on the phone with Hector's sister from Mexico. Most of his family lived there, and he had left her phone number on the note he'd written. As everyone was discussing the funeral arrangements, Jacob was feeling guilty about holding onto the secret about the homeless man Steve who was living in the church's mission home. Finally, Jacob shared the same story Steve had shared with him and Pastor Mark, with Hannah. It was shocking for Hannah to hear, but she still wanted to tell Steve that she forgave him for causing his wife to drink and drive, killing people in that major accident.

During their time at Pastor Mark's house, everyone managed to get things lined up for Hector's home going service that was going to be held right at the church. Jacob called Lisa to check on her and she was over Latasha's mother's house with her parents, making funeral arrangements for Latasha. Her funeral would be a day after Hector's. Lisa was very tired and very stressed out so Jacob left Pastor Mark's and then went to meet Lisa at her house after she and her parents had returned from Latasha's mother's house. Her parents had to cut their business travels short and fly back home after getting the news from

190

Lisa, so they were there to show their support to their daughter and Latasha's mother.

*****

Three days later, Corey met up with Spoon to go over the plan to take Detective Shan out. Corey did just as Mike had instructed him and waited for Jason to come out of the bank, then he tailed Jason with Spoon in the passenger seat. They rode for about three miles until they were finally able to catch Jason at a red light with no witnesses around to see what was about to go down. Corey hopped out and Spoon got behind the wheel of the car that Corey was driving. Corey opened Detective Shan's passenger side door and shot him right away, hitting him in the chest. Corey pulled the body into the passenger seat and then quickly ran around to the driver's side, jumped in the car, and drove off. Spoon was right behind him, holding up traffic to give Corey enough time to drive down to Hanson Gray River and dump Detective Shan's dead body right into the river.

Corey and Spoon drove to Light-skinned Chris' house and dropped off Jason's car so he could get rid of the car by chopping it down for parts and burning up the rest of it. Corey gave Light-skinned Chris $17,000 for doing the job then dropped Spoon off and gave him a $500,000 cut of the money. Spoon was one of Mike's day one soldiers, so according to him, it was only right that Spoon got a nice share of the money.

Corey called Mike on the burner phone. "Hey, everything is done and I am on my way to you now to bring

191

you the money. I will see you in the next five hours and you can let me know what is next.

"Alright li'l homie. You are doing very good and are a true soldier," said Mike.

Corey stopped at Fat Shakes and got a double cheeseburger with a blueberry and strawberry milkshake. After eating he headed straight to the highway to meet up with Mike in Miami. As Corey was driving he heard a song come on the radio that made him burst into tears. It was a song that Latasha loved and it reminded him of her.

"I don't care about anything or anyone now!" Corey said out loud to himself as he drove.

*****

Two days later, Corey was with Mike in Miami. They split up the money and stashed some of it away just in case the two of them needed to leave the country and be on the run. After splitting the money straight down the middle and paying other people who Mike put in position for their services, they both had $1.5 million to do whatever with. They both stashed their money in separate places and then took a little something to go to the mall with.

"Hey, Mike, with all this money we got are we going to put something towards Latasha's funeral?" Corey asked.

"No, li'l homie. Her mother has plenty of my money and it's more than enough," Mike replied. Mike and Corey headed to the mall to shop for some clothes to wear to Latasha's funeral. With all the drama that the two were in, Mike had been paying off Detective Shan to keep their names away from the murders they'd committed that could have put them away.

*****

As the mailman delivered the mail to everyone in the neighborhood, Pastor Mark stepped outside and got the package that Hector's letter said he would be receiving. Inside the package was a picture of Hector's daughter that he'd only seen once when she was five years old. He wanted Pastor Mark to deliver his will to her. It was the will to his estate, which was worth $14 million. He also left a check for Jacob with a note attached. The note read:

Dear Brother Jacob,

I told Pastor to tell you thanks, but I wanted to surprise you with a special thank you from my heart for leading me to God. Everything happens for a reason and I was really in the dark before I turned over my life to Jesus. I never felt so much peace come over me. I could not wait to share the Gospel of Jesus with the people who were lost in this world. Thanks to God, after all the evil and wicked things that I'd done to people, I did not have to wake up in hell. I have eternal life and I hope to see all you guys in the kingdom of heaven some day. Continue to be your own man and follow no one unless they are walking with the Lord. Here is a love offering to use for you to get married to that beautiful young woman of yours.

The check was for $3 million. In a separate letter to Pastor Mark, Hector apologized again for trashing the church and left him a check for $700,000 to put up for a second church. Pastor Mark called Hannah and asked her to wake up Jacob and meet him over his house because he had news for them both.

An hour and 45 minutes later, Hannah and Jacob showed up at Pastor Mark's house and were beyond happy at the news. The doorbell rang and it was Hector's sister Sarah from Mexico. She greeted and hugged everyone. Her husband Ricky was there as well, and they all prayed together and went over the final funeral arrangements since the next day would be Hector's home going service. Jacob was going to be doing the eulogy.

After more of Hector's family showed up from out of town, they all introduced themselves and spoke a little while with Pastor Mark, Jacob, and Hannah, sharing funny stories of the type of person Hector had been.

Two hours later, everyone left Pastor Mark's house and then Jacob drove to Lisa's house and spent a few hours with her.

"Hey babe, how are you holding up?" he asked her.

"I am holding up okay, Jacob, but why are you so busy worrying about Big Rome's home going when Latasha's home going is the next day? You should be over here helping me because my heart feels like it has gone from my body. I still can't believe that she is gone," said Lisa, crying with so much pain in her heart for losing someone who was just like her sister.

"I am sorry, babe, but I had to get the last things arranged for Hector's home going because I am preaching his eulogy. That man left me $3 million so now we can get married before we go back to school next month. We have more than enough money to pay wedding planners to speed the process up," said Jacob.

"Wow! Really? That would be nice to get married sooner because it will help clear my mind more if I am busy working and doing things to keep myself more occupied."

"We will talk more about this once the funerals are finished with."

"Let me ask you something, Jacob; do you think Latasha is in heaven?"

"I can't really answer that question, Lisa."

"Well, do you believe that Big Rome is in heaven?"

"Yeah, I do believe Hector made it in."

"Okay, I am a little confused because you just said you don't know about my girl Latasha but you believe Big Rome made it in."

"Look. I am just going to tell you straight up; Latasha's walk was not good with the Lord and you know that. She was smoking weed, having unprotected sex with Corey, and the two of you were always partying. That is not walking with the Lord. And before you try to go in on me telling me that I did these things, yes, I did, but I repented for my sins and did not keep repeating the same sins over and over again. The reason I am telling you I do not know about Latasha is because I do not know if she made it right with the Lord before her death. I know for sure about Hector because I was there when he accepted Jesus into his life. You can't just get into heaven without going through Jesus and this is where people in this world go wrong. They think they will be getting into heaven for their good deeds just by helping people out, like feeding the homeless and things like that. None of that means anything if the person does not confess with their mouth, believe in their heart, and ask Jesus to come into their lives. You must not die in sin; you have to die knowing you are forgiven of your sin, and that means dying while living for Jesus Christ. I, myself, had to repent to the Lord for what I did to Corey the other day because that was not of God at all and the next day all I kept asking myself was *how would Jesus have handled that?* Just sit here and really think about everything I just said. Because only you can really know for sure if you are living right and if you feel you are not right with the Lord I suggest that you give your life to Him. I love you and will talk to you later on. I have to go to the bank to meet my mom to deposit this check Hector left me. Pastor Mark should be on his way over to

Latasha's mom's house to set the final funeral arrangements for Latasha's home going. I know you will not be going to Hector's funeral and I do not expect you to. You may want to leave here and be over Latasha's mom's house within the next 25 minutes. That way you will get to the house around the time Pastor Mark shows up."

Jacob and Lisa hugged and kissed and said their goodbyes for the day. Jacob told her that he would see her after he was done with Hector's home going. He also told her to make sure she took the time to get some good rest when she came home from Latasha's mom's house.

Jacob got in his car and drove to the bank. He met Hannah there and deposited the check Hector had left him. The bank teller let him know that it would take up to ten business days for the check to clear because it was a very large amount and the funds needed to be verified.

*****

The next day came and everyone was at Hector's funeral. The church was so packed that everyone could not fit inside the church. They had put the main speakers in the front of the church entrance so the people standing outside could hear. You could see Big Rome's goons posted up all outside the church. There was a nice white horse and carriage parked right in front of the church to carry Hector's body to the cemetery after the home going service. Jacob brought the Word of the Lord and led a few of the goons to the Lord along with many other lost souls. The total number of people that gave their lives to the Lord was 86. They were all filled with the Holy Spirit.

After the service, everyone headed over to the cemetery as the pallbearers put Hector's body onto the back of the white horse-drawn carriage. Everything was so beautiful because everyone was dressed in all white.

After they buried Hector and put him into the ground, someone started screaming, "No, no, no! That's my little brother!" It was Sarah and she was taking her brother's death very hard. She knew that she would not see him ever again unless she made it into heaven.

Everyone met up at the repass and ate and mingled with each other. After everyone left to go home, Jacob stayed up reading the Bible and praying to the Lord. He needed to spend the rest of the day talking to God and needed to take a break from everyone. He'd been having stressful days and was just turning it over to Jesus. He prayed for four hours and then fell into a deep sleep.

*****

The next morning came and Jacob and Hannah got dressed to go to Latasha's funeral. He arrived at the church and it was full, but not as crowded as Hector's home going had been. Jacob sat next to Lisa as Hannah hugged Latasha's mom. Then they all went up to see her body for the last time. Latasha was in a white and gold coffin dressed in a cream suit. Pastor Mark went up to the pulpit and started peaching the Word of the Lord. About 27 minutes into his sermon, he looked up and saw Mike and Corey sitting in the back row. Mike pointed at Pastor Mark and tried to intimidate him by using his index finger and thumb to form a gun and pretending to shoot at him. Corey looked at Jacob with hatred in his eyes and shook his head.

"You see," said Pastor Mark, looking at Mike, "I am not going to let the devil put fear in my heart because I have Jesus. Just try me and find out when I hit you with the blood of Jesus. People these days have hearts so cold that they will do anything to get revenge. I am talking about wanting to get revenge so much that they would even risk getting their own family killed."

"Amen! You had better preach that Word, Pastor, preach! Hallelujah! Glory, glory, glory to the name of Jesus!" Jacob shouted out.

Mike and Corey walked up to Latasha's body and they both kissed her. Corey took a red rose and placed it inside her hand and then he threw on his shades and walked out of the church behind Mike. They hopped into an all-black limousine and the driver pulled off. While the funeral service was going on, Mike and Corey were in the limo plotting on how to take Pastor Mark and Jacob out. Now Corey had it out for Jacob too, thanks to Mike filling his head with a lot of hate and bad ideas about Jacob.

"This is the plan. Today is Friday so we are going to stay in town until Sunday. After the church service we will park 45 feet away from the church and we will make our move once some of the saints and security have left the church," said Mike.

After the powerful message that Pastor Mark had preached, Lisa went up and sang a song for her beloved friend. Afterwards, everyone headed over to the cemetery. At the burial, Lisa passed out and Jacob gave her some water to drink when she regained consciousness. She was taking Latasha's death very hard. Jacob saw Mike and

Corey drive by in the limo and Corey flashed his gun at Jacob. Jacob pulled Pastor Mark to the side to talk to him.

"Hey, Pastor, we need to carry some protection with us because I think now it's time we started watching our backs and each other's backs very closely. We have to make sure we're paying attention to our surroundings at all times," Jacob said.

"Yeah, young brother, you are right. We do, but remember that we both have something that they do not have. We have Jesus and He will not leave us or forsake us, for he is our protector," Pastor Mark said.

Everyone then went to Latasha's repass and Pastor Mark called Hannah and Lisa, and the three of them sat with Jacob to have a real talk about Mike and Corey plotting on them both.

"What? How do you know this for sure?" Hannah asked.

Jacob explained what had happened last week outside of Lisa's house.

"You did what, Jacob? What were you thinking? Why would you hit your own friend on the head with a gun and where did you get a gun from?" Hannah asked Jacob.

"I had one just to have and Corey was staring to act very shady towards me," Jacob said.

"Yes, Ms. Hannah, he was acting very funny because Jacob put two and two together and figured out that Corey called in the hit on Hector," said Lisa.

"What? So you mean to tell me the whole shootout at the lunch buffet was because of Corey?" Hannah asked.

"Yes, Hannah, and once Hector's crew found out that he was dead, they used an inside operator who had the drop on Latasha to kill her. I already knew the story because Jacob told me already, but we needed to find the right time to tell you. It was too much to tell you then with all the stuff that was already going on," said Pastor Mark.

"This is too much for me to handle even now. I mean, it is so much that I am speechless. I would never think in a million years that Corey would be involved in this crap. That kid would not hurt a fly," said Hannah.

"Well he would now and I saw it his eyes. It was that killer look; the look of a person that doesn't care about anything or anyone," said Jacob. "That's why we need to talk to you two. Because with Corey walking around in the streets like this he is liable to kill anyone who is in his way if he is trying to get at me. And, you already know what Mike is about. All that man wants is blood. Most of all, he wants Pastor Mark because he feels like he was betrayed."

"Why would he think something like that?" Hannah asked. "You know Pastor Mark and Mike stopped being friends years ago," she continued.

"Big Rome was trying to tell us before he passed that Mike was working with someone from the police department. Maybe Mike paid someone to stake out the church and then they saw Hector inside the church and went back telling Mike," Pastor Mark said.

"Remember Corey was with us in service when Hector gave his life to the Lord but when I asked him to go to the lunch buffet he would not go. He told me that he had some business to take care of and then he told me that he would catch me later on. After that is when all hell broke loose with the shootout at the lunch buffet and Hector being gunned down right outside of the place. That is why we need the two of you to leave town until at least Tuesday. I feel it in my spirit that Mike and Corey are going to try something this Sunday so we need to be prepared for whatever may come our way," said Jacob.

"Yes, young brother, we do, and we need to pray and ask the Lord for wisdom on what moves to make," Pastor Mark said.

"Okay, son, I will listen to you and go away until Tuesday. Lisa, will you be coming with me?" Hannah said.

"Yes, Ms. Hannah, I will be coming and while we are away maybe you can help me pick out my wedding dress. I will ask my mother to come along with us; that way we can all clear our heads and do some positive things. Pastor Mark and Jacob, you two just make sure you do not die because I do not want to go to any more funerals," said Lisa.

People started to leave Latasha's repass and head home. Jacob dropped his mother home and told her to start packing and Pastor Mark sent some of the church security to watch over Hannah while she was packing. Jacob drove Lisa to her house so she could pack her things. He then drove Lisa back over to his house and she spent the night there.

Hannah and Lisa, along with Lisa's mother, went away to Beverly Hills, California for their trip. They planned to shop for Lisa's wedding dress while they were there.

*****

Meanwhile, Mike was in a big meeting with his goons and had put Corey in charge as his top goon. It was time to get to work because Mike knew Pastor Mark before he became a pastor, and he knew that this could be a fight that he may not win.

*****

Pastor Mark called all his deacons and security to the church for their meeting. Jacob was praying for the church and they were reading their Bibles because they really did not want to hurt or kill anyone. They would rather made peace. Jacob, being the associate pastor, told everyone to brace themselves for what could be about to happen. All deacons and security were now fully aware of their roles in protecting the church. Everyone went home and went to bed after preparing in the five-hour meeting.

*****

It was now Sunday and everyone was on his or her way to the church to hear the Word of the Lord. Pastor Mark brought the Word as they had planned. He wanted Jacob to keep a watch and check on all the deacons and security to make sure they were at their posts. All the deacons and security were strapped with their guns and licensed to carry them. Pastor Mark gave the Word and everyone ate lunch at the church after the service ended. The deacons and security checked around the church and saw no sign of Mike. Pastor Mark sent his security home and then said prayers for a few people that needed prayer. Little did anyone know, Mike was parked up the street from the church in an old car with tinted windows so no one would be able to identify him.

As he watched the last few people leave the church, Mike started to make his way inside the church. Pastor Mark was sitting in the front row of the church with his back turned to Mike. Mike started slowly creeping up and Pastor Mark spoke out in a very soft and calm voice to Mike.

"Hey, Mike, I knew that you would show up because I know you well. You never want to change for the good. You always wanted to make bad decisions, but today you will learn to choose the right way. Before you try to take my life, you better think first and make the right decision for once. Today you have a choice to make, Mike, and that is choosing life or death. I am not just talking about life or death in the physical form, but I am talking about a spiritual life or death. Jesus said, *choose ye this day and you can have life with peace*, Mike," Pastor Mark said.

"You were never like me. You always were a coward and never had the heart for anything but your poor God," said Mike.

"Well, Mike, today you are about to find out how powerful God really is. I dare you to pull the trigger. Go on, bust your gun, dog. You will find that you are not the man you thought you were. You're calling me the coward but you are having a hard time pulling that trigger. The old me would have already blown your brains into lobster sauce, but I am not that man anymore, Mike. The reckless Mark died the day I gave my life over to the Lord. You know me and you know how I use to ride. Go ahead, bust your gun, and find out what will happen next," said Pastor Mark.

As Mike and the pastor traded words, Corey came around from the back of the church and ran right into Jacob.

"Corey, what is popping, man? Where do you think you're going? You will not bring evil in my house of worship. You see, I am ready to die tonight for the Lord. I will not let you finish what you started. You are the main reason why Latasha is dead right now. Come on, man, how many more people do you want to hurt before you finally end up dead? I'm done with all the talking. Do what you have to do," Jacob said.

Corey pulled the trigger, but the gun would not shoot. Mike pulled the trigger to shoot Pastor Mark, but his gun would not shoot either. It turned out that the security team had installed gun safety sensors in the church, a new piece of technology designed by a company named Rush

Link Computers LLC. The gun safety sensors were specially designed motion sensors that could detect any type of gun, old or new, and lock the metal inside to stop the click from kicking a single bullet when squeezing the trigger. They were originally designed for military use, but could now be used in churches to stop them from being robbed of their tithes and offering.

As Mike tried to pull the trigger on the gun, Pastor Mark grabbed him and slammed him into the ground then started kicking him.

"Didn't I tell you, punk, not to come up in my church with all this nonsense?" Pastor Mark said.

Mike reached into his right boot, grabbed a knife, and cut the pastor on his lower leg. Mike had a chance to get up and they began fighting to hand with punches flying back and forth.

Jacob and Corey were doing some scrapping of their own. They were going blow to blow but Corey started getting the best of Jacob. Jacob grabbed the small lamp from the top of the pulpit and cracked Corey right on his upper back, knocking him down to the floor.

"Corey, you never were a smart dude," said Jacob.

Pastor Mark and Mike continued fighting. They were both bloody as they traded punches and went toe to toe. They had both learned how to box from the same trainer, but Pastor Mark was a little more skilled with his hands, so as they continued to box, Mike tried to work his way to the pastor's body, and that is when Pastor Mark found his chance to go for the final blow. He punched Mike with a right jab then followed up with a left hook, putting him down for good.

The police had already been called. Corey tried to escape but tripped over a Bible that had fallen from the top of the pulpit when Jacob grabbed the lamp to hit him with. Finally, the police showed up and took Mike and Corey away, throwing them in jail without bail.

Jacob and Pastor Mark started to clean the church up after all the drama that went down. While cleaning up, Pastor Mark found Mike's fake ID with his new Miami address on it. He couldn't believe Mike was using his name on his fake ID.

Jacob got a call from Hannah; she wanted to check on him. He told her what had happened and that everything was okay now. Hannah told him that Lisa had found her wedding dress.

"That is great, Mom. I can't wait to see it when you get back," he said.

"Nice try, son, but you will only see the dress on your wedding day," Hannah told him.

*****

One month later, that day had come. All of Jacob and Lisa's family and friends were there to see their beautiful day. Pastor Mark was at the altar with Lisa and Jacob, who had just exchanged their wedding vows.

"You may now kiss the bride," Pastor Mark said, and Jacob grabbed Lisa and kissed her as if Jesus was going to crack the sky today. "I would like to announce for the first time in public, Mr. and Mrs. Justice!"

The bride and groom marched away with so much joy and happiness. They took pictures and then turned and looked at one another.

"Something doesn't feel right," they said to each other at the same time.

"It feels weird without Corey being by my side as my best man. I always thought he would be here for this because this is what we talked about as little kids." Jacob said.

"Yeah, I feel very weird too without Latasha being right beside me as my maid of honor. I know she is looking down on me and very proud of me though," said Lisa.

Everyone made their way to the wedding reception and the entire bridal party was announced, followed by the bride and groom. The bride and groom had their first dance and then Lisa danced with her father. Right after that, Jacob danced with Hannah in his arms and they started to talk about all that God had blessed them with.

"Hey, son, I am very proud of you because you have become a mighty man of God. You're about to finish school in a few more years and will be ready to take over your father's church. You will someday become a father and you will be held responsible," Hannah said.

"I know, Mom, and I will be a good dad to my kids. I just pray and hope I have a boy for my first child."

"Just pray and ask God for a boy and you will get a boy. That is what your father did and then came you. What will you name your son if God blesses you with a boy? Will you name him Jacob the third?"

"No, I will name him Josiah."

"Wow, Josiah is a great name and the Bible talks about Josiah being a king. That is a very strong and powerful name. I like that, son."

The bride and groom went and sat down to listen to some of the friends give speeches and then they lifted their glasses for a toast.

"To Lisa and Jacob, may your marriage last forever and may you always keep God in your marriage. Remember, nothing is too hard for God," said Pastor Mark.

Jacob took the garter from under Lisa's dress, and when he threw it up, Pastor Mark caught it. Lisa threw the bouquet and Hannah caught it. Everyone hit the dance floor and danced, talked, and had fun with each other. Finally, the bride and groom cut their wedding cake and then they walked around to thank everyone for their support.

After everyone left and went home for the night, Jacob and Lisa went to their hotel suite. Jacob was so happy to be able to make love to Lisa and not feel convicted with God for sleeping around unmarried that he went way beyond. They enjoyed making love with each other so much that they could not wait until the next day to go on their honeymoon.

They headed out to the Dominican Republic the very next day. Once they finally landed they could not believe how beautiful the place was and the things they were seeing for the first time in their lives. They hung out, held hands, talked, and had so much fun while on their honeymoon. They went to a fancy restaurant in the all-inclusive resort they were staying in.

"I love you, Jacob, and really thank God for you," Lisa told him.

"I love to you too, Lisa, and thank God for you. Look how far we've come. It seems just like yesterday me, you, Corey, and Latasha were all hanging out at your house in your movie theater," Jacob replied.

"Aww, don't bring it up. You are going to make me cry. I think about those moments every now and then."

*****

Seven years later...

Jacob and Lisa were now 27 years old and Lisa was seven months pregnant with their baby boy, Josiah Jacob Justice. Jacob and Lisa had finished school and Lisa was now the owner of her own Gospel network that played all types of Gospel movies to help lead people to Jesus Christ. Jacob was the pastor of the church his father had passed down to him through Pastor Mark and he was ready to start building more churches to start spreading the Gospel of Jesus Christ.

"Apostle Mark, God bless you today. It is good to see you, brother," said Jacob.

"It is always an honor to see you, Pastor Jacob. Your mother and father would be so proud to see what God has done for you."

"Yeah, I really miss my mom. She was a very good woman. I am just glad that I followed the way of the Lord. I could have gone the other way and been dead or locked up like Mike and Corey."

"Oh, I almost forgot, I got a letter from Corey in the mail. Come on, Apostle Mark, you're reading my mail now," Jacob laughed.

"No, my brother, I just thought I would grab it just in case you decided to throw it in the trash. I think you should write him because this could be your chance to win him over to Jesus."

"I will take the time to write him when I take a break tomorrow."

"So who you like this year in football?"

"The Gold Ducks are looking nice this year but they just need to get a quarterback that can take few hits and not go down so quick."

"Yeah, you're right about that, Pastor Jacob, but he is nice inside the pocket. Well, are you ready to bring the Word today, Pastor?"

"Yes, I already was on my knees praying to ask God what to preach about."

Steve walked in to see if Jacob was almost ready.

"Minister Steve, how are you doing today?" Jacob asked him.

"I am blessed, my brothers. It feels good to be in the presence of the Lord. You are up in ten minutes, Pastor Jacob."

"Okay, cool, do you have the cameras ready to record. And what about the lighting?"

"Everything is all set and ready to start."

Pastor Jacob walked to the pulpit from the back of the church as he was streaming live and broadcasting on Lisa's cable network. "Hallelujah! Glory to God! Today I want to share a Word from the Lord that talks about living to fulfill God's works. If you have your Bibles with you today I want you to turn with me to the book of Colossians 1:10. Say *amen* when you've got the scripture. It reads *that ye might walk worthy of the Lord unto all pleasing, being fruitful in every good work, and increasing in the knowledge of God.* What is this scripture talking about? It is talking about how we have to walk worthy unto the Lord and we must do what pleases him, not man. We, as the people of God, must fulfill the works of the Lord by spreading the Word of God. The more of the Word of God being spread, the harder it becomes for the devil to come in because now more people have the knowledge of God. That is why we have to do the work of God to complete the assignments that He assigns for each one of us to do. We are not here just to be here. God has us here for a reason, and that's to do His work, winning people over to Him. The more people that give their lives to Jesus Christ, the less people that are out in the world living for the devil. It was never about you. Now look to your neighbor and say *it was never about you.* We have to stand up for the Lord and meet Him face to face to let Him know what we plan to do for Him today. He gave us life. Come on now, the least we can do for Him is to go out and share the Gospel with people. We cannot just sit here and be selfish with the Gospel. We have to go out and spread it out to all the nations. That is what Jesus told us to do before He went up to heaven."

Pastor Jacob preached a heart-filling sermon and later decided to read Corey's letter before he left the church:

Dear Jacob,

I am sorry for how things went down. That was not the real me. It was nothing but the devil taking over my mind. I finally gave my life to Jesus and live for Him now. I heard that you and Lisa got married and you have a boy on the way. Congratulations. I am sorry to hear about Ms. Hannah. She was like another mother to me. Please pray for me and pray for my mother also. She just had three strokes and is not doing too well. I feel bad that I am not out there to help her. Mike was three cells next to me on the same block, but he got transferred because he stabbed someone and hurt him very badly. Mike is losing his mind being locked up, so pray for him too. I pray and hope you decide to write me back but if not, I understand.

Corey

After Jacob read the letter, he started to write a letter back to Corey:

Dear Corey,

You are still my brother and most of all, you are my new brother in Christ. I think about you all the time and I want nothing but the best for you, bro. I pray that the Lord keeps you protected while you're in jail and will pray that you get an early release. Remember that if you trust and believe in

God all things are possible. It is never too late for you to live a good life and do the right thing. Thanks for congratulating me on my wedding and on my unborn baby boy. I just wish you were here to experience all of this. We have a few new churches and Lisa has her own Gospel cable network. I will pray and visit to check on your mom. Just send me her address when you write me back because I know she moved four years ago. I will pray for you and try to find the time to visit you. God bless you.

Jacob

*****

A few months later, Lisa delivered a healthy baby boy. Jacob was so happy to meet his son face to face for the first time. Apostle Mark visited along with a few other church family and friends and they all prayed to thank the Lord for the new life that was added to the family.

"Thank you, Jesus." Jacob looked to the clouds outside of his window. "Mom and Dad, I will see you both when God calls me there, but I do not plan on going now," he laughed. Jacob walked down the hall to get something to drink and his phone rang.

"*You have a collect call from an inmate*, Corey. Press one if you choose to accept. Press two if you choose not to accept," the recorded voice said. Jacob pressed one to accept Corey's call.

"Hey, listen, I just got the word," Corey said, sounding panicked.

"You got the word on what? Calm down; I can't really hear what you're trying to tell me. Now take a deep breath and tell me what's going on," said Jacob.

"Bro, it's Mike. He escaped while he was being transferred to another prison. It seemed as if he wanted to be moved to other jails so he could find his chance to break out."

"You have two minutes remaining," the operator's voice said in the background. "I got the word that Mike is coming straight for you and your people."

"Where did you hear that?"

"Someone that I am very cool with."

"You have 45 seconds remaining."

"Look, we're not worried. We've got Jesus on our side. If Mike comes our way he had better come correct."

"My brother, I have to go. The phone is about to hang up on me. Just watch your back and send me a letter."

"Alright, bro, you stay blessed up."

"You do the same and remember, watch your back."

Jacob got his soda and walked back into Lisa's hospital room. "Apostle Mark, can I talk to you in private real quick?" Jacob asked him.

"What's up, Pastor Jacob? What's on your mind?"

"I just got a call from Corey in jail and he just gave me the word that Mike broke out of jail. He is coming right for the both of us as soon as he is settled."

"Pastor Jacob, I am not worried and you should not be worried because the Lord will protect us. When Mike comes I will be ready because he is the gangster and we are the preachers and in the end, good shall always overcome evil. Amen!"

To Be Continued ...

Look out for

The Gangster is Out for the Preachers

Coming Soon!

Follow

THE GANGSTER

VS.

THE PREACHER

 King Rush Publishing

 KingRush35

 KingRush35

Website: www.kingrushpublishing.com

E-mail: contact@kingrushpublishing.com

www.ingramcontent.com/pod-product-compliance
Lightning Source LLC
Chambersburg PA
CBHW072050170626
46813CB00004B/1282